Samantha had tears in her eyes . . .

Wonder's Pride fought back with a vengeance, pouring out more speed, and the two horses roared down the stretch.

"A breathtaking stretch drive!" the announcer screamed. "Wonder's Pride not giving an inch! Super Value, the fresh horse who hasn't raced in a month, continuing to challenge on the outside. Now he gets a nose in front. But Wonder's Pride comes back at him to get *his* nose in front. A fight to the finish here! A true show of courage! And Ashleigh Griffen hasn't touched him with her whip! They're at the wire! Too close to call . . . a photo finish! An unbelievable finish to this year's Triple Crown!"

Samantha had tears in her eyes. Pride had just demonstrated every ounce of heart he possessed.

Don't miss these exciting books from
HarperPaperbacks!

Collect all the books in the
THOROUGHBRED series:

THOROUGHBRED

SAMANTHA'S PRIDE

JOANNA CAMPBELL

HarperPaperbacks

A Division of HarperCollins*Publishers*

HarperPaperbacks *A Division of* HarperCollins*Publishers*
  10 East 53rd Street, New York, N.Y. 10022

Copyright © 1993 by Daniel Weiss Associates, Inc., and
Joanna Campbell.

Cover art copyright © 1993 Daniel Weiss Associates, Inc.

All rights reserved. No part of this book may be used or repro-
duced in any manner whatsoever without written
permission of the publisher, except in the case of brief
quotations embodied in critical articles and reviews. For information address Daniel Weiss Associates, Inc., 33 West 17th
Street, New York, New York 10011.

Produced by Daniel Weiss Associates, Inc., 33 West 17th Street,
New York, New York 10011.

A digest-size edition of this title was published by
HarperPaperbacks in August 1993.

First rack-size edition printing: January 1995

Printed in the United States of America

HarperPaperbacks and colophon are trademarks of
HarperCollins*Publishers*

10 9 8 7 6 5 4 3 2 1

SAMANTHA'S PRIDE

1

A CROWD OF REPORTERS SURGED AROUND SAMANTHA McLean as she led Wonder's Pride away from the winner's circle. The elegant chestnut Thoroughbred had just won the Fountain of Youth Stakes at Gulfstream Park in Florida, defeating some of the best three-year-olds in the country!

"What did you think of the race?" a reporter yelled out to Charlie Burke, the old trainer who had helped with Pride's training and was walking with Samantha and Pride to the backside. "What's the likelihood of his heading to the Kentucky Derby and the Triple Crown?"

"Race was just fine," Charlie answered with his usual brevity, resettling his floppy felt hat on his gray hair. "Too soon to tell about the Triple Crown.

It's only February. A lot could happen before May."

"He may have missed the Breeder's Cup Juvenile," another reporter called out, "but he's still looking like the best three-year-old this year."

"Yup," Charlie replied.

"And you're not ready to commit to the Derby?" the reporter said with astonishment. "When's his next race?"

"Not sure."

Samantha chuckled at Charlie's terseness. The reporters knew Charlie and should have known better than to think they'd get much information from him. But Pride certainly *had* come off his winter layoff raring to go. He'd run in an allowance race earlier in the month and had walked away from the field—and now he'd done the same in the Fountain of Youth! Samantha laid a loving hand on his sleek, muscular neck, and he gently lipped her thick mane of bright red hair in answer. At fifteen, Samantha was five foot four, slim, and totally involved in Pride's training. She had dreamed of seeing Pride in the winner's circle since the day Ashleigh Griffen, the colt's half owner and jockey, had asked Samantha to be his groom. Now, nearly two years later, Samantha rode him in almost all of his workouts at their home farm, Whitebrook, and had even greater dreams for his future.

As they neared the barn area, the reporters

drifted off, but grooms and other stablehands began waving and calling out their congratulations. Yvonne Ortez, Samantha's best friend, came rushing up to them, her straight black hair flying back away from her face and her dark eyes sparkling. She loved being at the track as much as Samantha.

"I never thought I'd get through that crowd," Yvonne cried. "You should hear what they're saying about Pride! It was such an incredible race!"

"It sure was," Samantha said, turning her green eyes toward Pride. "And Ashleigh said he did it all by himself. She didn't even have to ask him for more in the stretch. He just took off."

"Where *is* Ashleigh?" Yvonne asked.

"Still changing out of her silks," Samantha answered. "She should be here in a minute, though."

They had reached Pride's stall block, and Samantha stopped the colt in the yard outside. "First I'll sponge you off, big boy," she said to the colt. "Then we'll take you for a long walk to cool you out." Pride bobbed his head as if he understood her every word.

Yvonne grabbed a bucket and started filling it with water from a nearby faucet. Samantha held Pride as Charlie slid off the lightweight sheet covering the colt's back. He ran his hands over Pride's slender legs and checked his feet.

"Looks good to me," Charlie said after he had

3

given Pride a thorough inspection. "See if there's any stiffness after you walk him, but I don't think there will be."

Samantha wet a sponge in the bucket Yvonne had filled and ran it over the colt's back. He hadn't worked up an excessive sweat in the sixty-five-degree February Florida weather, but his coat was darkened, and he grunted in pleasure as the cool water coursed over him.

"That's better, isn't it?" Samantha smiled and reached down to wet her sponge again as Yvonne worked on the colt's other side.

"Call me when you're done cooling him out," Charlie said, "and I'll have another look."

As Charlie shuffled off, Yvonne turned to Samantha. "How are you feeling? Excited?"

"You're not kidding! Ashleigh told me how crazy it can get when your horse starts winning big races—he got a lot of attention when he won the Champagne last fall, but it was nothing like this. People are really getting excited about the Triple Crown."

Yvonne grinned. "Yeah, and he could be running in it."

"Every owner and trainer's dream is to run a horse in the Kentucky Derby," Samantha said with a touch of awe in her voice. "I know that's how my father feels. And here I am grooming and helping train a horse who might actually make it there!"

4

"I'm so glad we had winter vacation this week, and I was able to drive down to Florida with you guys," Yvonne said. "I've had so much fun!"

"Well, Mike really appreciated your helping him out with the horses," Samantha told her. "And it has been fun, hasn't it?"

"Incredible, and this is just the beginning!"

Samantha laughed at her friend's exuberance. It *was* just the beginning of what she hoped would be a wonderful three-year-old season for Pride. "I can't believe that less than a year ago, Clay Townsend was ready to sell out his interest in Pride," Samantha said.

"I know," Yvonne agreed. "Things sure are different—but so much better now that you, your father, Charlie, and Pride are all at Whitebrook. And you don't have to be around Brad Townsend anymore."

Samantha wrinkled her nose at the thought of Clay Townsend's arrogant son. Until the previous spring Samantha and her father had lived on the Townsends' prestigious breeding and training farm, Townsend Acres. "I could hardly stand being around Brad, especially after he tried to fire my father," Samantha said. "And he was the one who really wanted to sell Pride."

"You're lucky he doesn't come over to Whitebrook and bother you," Yvonne said.

"Not yet, anyway. Mr. Townsend has left

Pride's training in Ashleigh and Charlie's hands, but if Pride does really well, Brad will probably start interfering again."

Samantha eased a sweat strap over Pride's damp coat, removing the excess moisture. Then she dried him with towels and threw the light sheet over his back. As she did, Ashleigh Griffen and her long-time boyfriend, Mike Reese, came over to join them. Ashleigh's shoulder-length dark hair was still damp from the shower she'd taken after changing out of her jockey's silks.

"You're looking good, boy!" Ashleigh said as she threw her arms around Pride's neck and gave him a hug. "What a race. I'm so proud of you!"

The colt nickered his appreciation.

"Did you get mobbed by reporters?" Samantha asked.

"I sure did, and I guess Mr. Townsend's been giving out plenty of interviews. I hear we're running Pride in the Florida Derby and Blue Grass." Ashleigh frowned. "Nice of him to tell me about it."

"I thought you were considering both races," Samantha said.

"Charlie and I have talked about it, but nothing was ever definite."

"Townsend is probably just trying to get all the publicity he can for Townsend Acres," Mike said. "They need it, and he knows Pride can bring it to them."

Ashleigh shrugged. "Maybe I'm overreacting, but I can't help wondering if I'm going to be cut out of the decision-making—now that Pride's doing so well."

"Mr. Townsend wouldn't do that," Yvonne said. "Would he?"

"He's always been pretty decent," Ashleigh answered thoughtfully, "but Townsend Acres still isn't doing that well financially. The more Pride races and wins, the better it is for them."

"You're counting chickens before they're hatched," Charlie said, walking up to hear Ashleigh's last comments. "Townsend was telling the reporters what they wanted to hear." He looked at Samantha. "You going to get this colt walked today, or not?"

Samantha flushed. She should have been cooling Pride, not standing around talking. She quickly started to lead the colt off, and Yvonne followed behind her.

"Mike and I are taking you, Yvonne, and Charlie out to eat tonight, to celebrate," Ashleigh called after her. "We'll meet you back here. It'll have to be an early night, though, since we're leaving for Lexington first thing in the morning."

"See you later, then," Samantha answered.

They arrived back in Lexington late on Sunday night. Both Samantha and Yvonne were feeling a little dazed and tired from the long trip when they met at their lockers at Henry Clay High School on Monday morning. Samantha had just closed her locker door when Maureen O'Brian hurried up to them. Maureen was on the school newspaper staff with Samantha and was a very conscientious feature editor. The previous year she had asked Samantha to write a monthly article on horse racing, since it was such a big industry in Kentucky and Samantha had so much firsthand experience.

"So did you watch Pride race?" Yvonne asked Maureen.

Maureen, small and pixielike, pushed her thick glasses up the bridge of her nose. "Of course I watched the race! I'm impressed! And I saw Clay Townsend interviewed. Are you really going to the Triple Crown?" she asked Samantha excitedly.

"It's too soon to tell, but I sure hope so," Samantha said. "I get excited just thinking about it."

"Well, so would I," Maureen answered. "Listen, you're going to have to devote at least one of your articles to the Triple Crown. We could run it in late spring, just before the Kentucky Derby. Maybe you could write something about your experiences at the big races. You're going, aren't you?"

Samantha laughed. "You're really jumping ahead, Maureen. I guess I'll be going, if Pride goes, but I'm not even sure he'll be racing."

Maureen waved her hand carelessly. "Oh, I'm

8

sure he'll run, especially after watching him race this weekend. I mean, he left the rest of them in the dust." Maureen flipped open her notebook. "Now, let me look at the schedule."

As she did, Tor Nelson walked up to the girls. The smiling, blond-haired senior was Yvonne's riding instructor at the local stable, and Samantha and Yvonne had both become good friends with him. "Great race!" he said to Samantha. "It must have been super actually being there."

Samantha returned his smile. "It was! And now we'll start training for the next one."

"Sounds like you're going to have a busy spring, but we've still got to get you over to the stable for that free jumping lesson I promised," he reminded her.

"Right!" Yvonne cried. "Don't worry, Tor, I'm keeping after her. I know she's going to have at least a week off from training, since Pride will have to be rested." She grinned devilishly at Samantha. "I'll get her over one afternoon."

"I promised I'd come, didn't I?" Samantha protested. "And I will." She refused to admit to either of them that she was a little hesitant. She was an accomplished rider, but she'd never jumped. And though she wasn't afraid, she didn't want to look like an awkward beginner. Yvonne had been doing extremely well in her jumping lessons, which she'd started the year before, and Tor was an expert who had his own Thoroughbred jumper and competed in the top shows.

"How about Wednesday afternoon, then?" Tor said. "I have a free hour."

"She'll be there," Yvonne said, smiling cheerfully.

"I guess I will," Samantha answered, giving her pushy friend a dark look. Then she laughed. "Yeah, I'll be there."

"Okay, I've worked out the schedule," Maureen said, scribbling in her notebook. "You can write a lead-up to the Derby for the April issue. Then in May, you can write a firsthand account of the Preakness and the Belmont."

"The Belmont's not till June," Samantha said.

"Oh." Maureen frowned. "Well, you can give some background about the Belmont, but definitely write about the Preakness in detail—you know, the atmosphere, the crowds and stuff."

"You're pretty confident," Samantha teased. "We may not even be there."

"Oh, you will be," Maureen said firmly, "after Pride wins the Derby."

When Samantha walked up Whitebrook's drive from the school bus that afternoon, she saw Clay Townsend's red Jeep Cherokee parked in the drive. He was over a lot now that Pride was back in training again. Samantha had heard from

Charlie, who spoke frequently to Hank, the head groom at Townsend Acres, that things were still pretty grim at the huge breeding and training farm. They hadn't replenished the stock they had sold at auction the year before, and although they had a new crop of decent yearlings and were looking forward to the foaling season ahead, they only had twenty horses in training, and not many showed potential. It seemed that most of the Townsends' hopes rested on Pride, and the foal his dam, Wonder, was due to deliver that spring.

Samantha hurried across the drive toward the small cottage she and her father shared. To her left was the modest white farmhouse where Mike and his father lived. To her right were three stabling barns, various outbuildings, and the mile training oval. Behind the barns was Charlie's cottage, which he shared with Len, Mike's stable manager, and surrounding it all were acres of white-fenced paddocks. Whitebrook was a small operation compared to Townsend Acres, but it was growing and gaining a good reputation, particularly at the Kentucky tracks. With Samantha's father's help, Mike was taking in young horses to train in addition to the half-dozen actively racing horses he owned himself.

Samantha hurried into the cottage and up the stairs to change out of her school clothes. The cottage was small, with a living room and eat-in

11

kitchen downstairs and two bedrooms and a bath upstairs, but to Samantha it was a real home—bigger than the apartment she and her father had shared at Townsend Acres. Before her father had taken the job of assistant trainer at Townsend Acres nearly three years before, the McLeans had moved constantly from track to track, wherever her father could find a job. The lifestyle had been hard for Samantha. She'd never lived in any area long enough to make really good friends. Of course, she'd always had the horses, which she loved. But then her mother had been killed in a training accident, and Samantha's world had fallen apart. Only recently had Samantha started to feel a sense of security again, though she still missed her mother terribly.

She laid her books on top of the small desk in her room and quickly changed out of her clothes. Then she ran back downstairs, grabbed an apple from the bowl on the kitchen table, and headed out to the stables to see Pride. He'd come out of the Fountain of Youth in amazingly good shape, and Charlie and Ashleigh had been pleased.

She saw her father standing at one of the paddock rails, watching several two-year-olds cavorting on the still-brown grass. His auburn hair shone in the weak February sunlight. Soon spring would arrive. The grass would start greening, and the crocuses would bloom. Samantha couldn't wait.

She hurried into the stable building and heard Charlie and Mr. Townsend talking.

"I think we should have kept him down in Florida," Mr. Townsend was saying. "He could have stayed in training at Gulfstream and been right there for the Florida Derby."

"Sure," Charlie answered brusquely, "I could have stayed with him, but Ashleigh's got college classes, and you know the colt stays more relaxed and trains better when he's on home turf and Sammy's around to groom and ride him. We can bring him back down if your mind's made up about running him in the Florida Derby."

Samantha paused in the aisle, but she could see the scowl on Charlie's face.

"I thought that was decided on a long time ago," Mr. Townsend answered.

Charlie rubbed his chin. "The race is only a little over two weeks away. Then you want to run him again in the Blue Grass the second week in April."

"The colt's in top form," Mr. Townsend said. "Look at the performance he put in last weekend."

"I'm just thinking ahead to the Triple Crown," Charlie said. "It'll be pretty grueling."

"I know it'll be tough, but I'm sure the colt is up to it."

Charlie shrugged.

"Well, I've got to get back to the farm," Mr.

Townsend said. "When are you going to start working him again?"

"Friday or Saturday."

"I'll be here." Clay Townsend turned to leave. As he passed Samantha in the aisle, he smiled. "Hello, Sammy. He's looking very perky. Take good care of him."

"I always do, Mr. Townsend," she answered. Then she walked up the aisle to Charlie. "He's definitely racing in the Derby?" she asked, wide-eyed.

"Sounds like. Of course, if he throws in a bad performance in the next two races, Townsend could change his mind."

"He won't throw in a bad performance!" Samantha said loyally. "So, has Ashleigh agreed to his race schedule?"

Charlie nodded. "It's a little hard not to get Derby fever. It's catching."

Yes, Samantha agreed silently as Charlie shuffled off, it certainly *was* catching. She went to Pride's stall and grinned at the horse as he thrust his head over the half-door. "Did you hear that? They're heading you toward the Derby, boy! We're going places!"

ON WEDNESDAY AFTERNOON, SAMANTHA WALKED WITH Yvonne from school to the riding stable a half-mile away.

"This is great," Yvonne said. "If you start jumping, maybe we can even ride in a show together."

Samantha smiled, but her thoughts were a million miles away. Since she'd found out Pride was definitely headed toward the Kentucky Derby, she'd been breathless with excitement. Already Samantha could imagine Pride standing in the winner's circle with a blanket of roses draped over his shoulders. The thought sent shivers down her spine.

Tor was waiting as Samantha and Yvonne entered the long stable building, which had a large, dirt-floored indoor ring at one end. The stable was more quiet than usual, since there wasn't a class in progress, but several private owners were grooming their boarded horses and two grooms were bustling about.

Tor had a bay gelding in crossties and was tacking him up. He looked up and smiled as Samantha and Yvonne approached. "You're right on time," he said. "This is Cocoa. I thought he'd make a good mount for you since you're already an experienced rider. He's got some spunk, but he's well-trained and won't pull any funny stuff."

Samantha smiled at Tor and patted the bay's shoulder. He turned his head as far as the crossties would allow and eyed her, snorting softly.

"We're going to be friends," Samantha said to the horse, "and you can teach me what jumping's all about."

"He's been doing it for a long time," Tor said.

Samantha sat down on a nearby tack box and pulled on her boots as Tor finished tightening Cocoa's saddle girth. "Okay, tell me what I'm supposed to do," she said, rising and putting on her hat.

Tor unclipped the crossties and started leading Cocoa down the aisle toward the indoor ring.

"You're not going to start her with the real simple stuff, like you do with the regular classes, are you?" Yvonne asked.

"I think Sammy already knows how to post to

the trot and what leads are all about," Tor said, grinning at Samantha.

She smiled back. "I think I do."

"I thought we could start warming him up with some figure eights, go over your jump and hunt seats, then try some cavalletis—see how it goes."

Samantha already knew what the terms meant, partially from experience and partially from listening to Yvonne go on for hours about her lessons. Tor held Cocoa's head as Samantha fastened her chin strap and mounted. Then she checked the girth and adjusted the stirrup length.

"Too short," Tor told her. "You want the iron to hit your ankle bone when your leg is extended. You're not galloping horses right now. You'll need more leg around the horse when you're jumping."

Samantha let the stirrups down one hole, feeling a little stupid. She should have known that. It was just habit for her to ride with slightly short stirrups.

She settled in the saddle and picked up the reins. As always, she felt perfectly at ease. She dropped her heels automatically, so that the balls of her feet rested on the stirrup irons and her toes pointed up.

"After you warm him up," Tor said, "do some figure eights at a posting trot, then at a canter. You don't need me to explain?" he asked.

Samantha shook her head and started Cocoa

forward at a walk. Her back and shoulders were straight, and her head was up, her gaze directed between his ears. Then she urged him into a trot, posting in the saddle as he lifted his outside shoulder. He had an energetic gait and seemed eager and willing, although his movement couldn't be compared to Pride's smooth and powerful strides.

"That's it, boy," she said after circling the ring twice. "Now let's try some figure eights." She circled him evenly around the top half of the ring, then gently reined him in toward the center. At the point where the two circles of the eight would connect, she sat a half-beat in the saddle, then rose with his opposite shoulder as they completed the bottom circle of the eight.

Cocoa was definitely well-schooled, she thought as he went through the exercise with experienced ease. After several figure eights at a trot, Samantha collected the reins and gave him the signal to canter, sitting deep in the saddle. He changed gaits without a falter and led out correctly with his inside foreleg. When she reached the center of the eight, she stopped him for the briefest instant, then gave him the command to canter again, this time on the opposite lead. He changed leads and cantered on. Since racehorses ran counterclockwise around the track, and only changed leads when they were coming down the stretch, Samantha had more experience working horses on the left lead.

With concentration, though, she didn't have any trouble adjusting to the quicker lead changes of the figure eights.

After finishing three figures at a canter, she glanced over at Tor and saw him motion for her to pull Cocoa up. Yvonne was smiling from where she stood at the side of the ring. "How'd I look?" Samantha asked Tor as she walked the gelding over to him.

He smiled. "Do you have to ask? Teaching you is a little different than teaching most of my first classes. We may even try a jump today. Let me run though the jump seat first, though. As you're approaching a jump," he explained, "you're going to be lifting just slightly out of the saddle, back and shoulders still straight. The jump seat takes some of the stress off the horse, so that you're lifting with him when he gathers himself. You do a version of it when you're galloping horses, although you don't want to lift that far out of the saddle."

"That's kind of what I thought," Samantha said. She lifted herself just slightly out of the saddle, keeping her heels down. "Like this?"

"Looks good," Tor answered, studying her. "Take him around at a trot and canter, so you're sure you have the feel of it. Then we'll trot him through the cavalettis I've set up over there." He motioned to the top center of the ring.

Samantha nodded, turned Cocoa, and started trotting him around the perimeter of the ring as she lifted into the jump seat. After one lap, she cantered him, thinking that so far the lesson was fairly easy. Of course, she knew she shouldn't let herself get too confident. What she was doing was stuff she'd already done before. Jumping would be different.

"Okay," Tor called, "trot him through the cavalettis. Stay in your jump seat. Start him from the bottom."

She turned Cocoa up the center of the ring toward the six evenly spaced poles laid on the dirt floor. She kept her head up and back straight as they bounced through. Again Cocoa's experience helped her. He lifted his feet high and cleanly over the poles. They went through twice more before Tor signaled Samantha to stop. Yvonne gave Samantha a grin and a thumbs-up.

"Do you want to try a jump?" Tor asked.

"Sure," Samantha said, feeling the first touch of nervousness.

"We'll start with a low X." Tor motioned to Yvonne, who collected two posts from the dismantled jumps at the end of the ring. She positioned them, then crossed two poles and braced them in the lower notches of the posts.

"Approach at a trot in your jump seat," Tor explained. "Head always up, looking toward the jump. *Never* look down, or you'll throw off your horse and yourself. You'll have to concentrate on your timing and get the feel of when to jump. If you signal your mount to jump too far from the fence, you'll be lucky if you clear it. If you signal too close, the horse will pop over, land off balance, and probably unseat you. When you feel you're at the right takeoff point, squeeze with your legs and give the horse rein, so he can freely extend his neck."

Samantha had listened carefully, then nodded.

"Circle him around the end of the ring and approach from that direction," Tor added. "Remember, keep your head up and look toward the jump you're approaching."

Samantha heeled Cocoa into a trot and circled him. Then she straightened the horse and headed toward the low X at a trot. She lifted into her jump seat and watched as Cocoa's strides brought them closer. She concentrated and tried to judge when to signal Cocoa to jump. A little bit closer, she thought. Then she squeezed with her legs and gave rein. The horse lifted over the small obstacle, but even before they landed, with Cocoa's rear hoofs barely clearing the low X, she knew she'd goofed.

"Too soon," she said to Tor as she circled back.

He nodded. "If it had been a higher jump, he definitely would have taken down a rail."

21

"I'm beginning to see what you mean about feeling it. It felt wrong before we'd even landed."

"Try again," Tor told her.

She did, again, and again, until she was sure she had the timing just right. Then Tor added another low fence—just a single rail set only a foot or so off the ground—several strides from the crossbar. He instructed her to land off the first, look straight ahead to the second, and continue at a canter, counting strides. She did both fences cleanly, but Samantha didn't realize how hard she'd been concentrating until she rode Cocoa over to Tor and Yvonne.

Yvonne was laughing. "You should see your face, Sammy! You're scowling so hard, your forehead's all wrinkled."

"I am?" Samantha said in surprise. "It's just that I wanted to get it right. It's not as easy as I thought. I mean, it's not like riding Pride in a workout. On the oval I don't even have to think about what I'm doing—I just do it. But with jumping, I have to think all the time."

"With practice it'll come as naturally as riding in a workout," Tor assured her. "Just give it a little time. For your next lesson, we'll try three fences."

"Oh, we will, will we?" Samantha said, grinning.

Tor looked up at her with a bright gleam in his blue eyes. "You did great today."

"Thanks," Samantha said, a flush rising up in her cheeks.

"You can cool him out now," he said to her. "We didn't give him much of a workout, though, so he won't need much walking." He patted Cocoa's shoulder.

"You know, Tor," Samantha said hesitantly, "I don't know if I can afford regular lessons."

"We'll talk about that later," he said. "I'll see you back in the stable. I have to get horses ready for my next class."

As he strode off, Samantha dismounted and pulled up the stirrups. Yvonne joined her as she started walking Cocoa around the ring. "You really did do great," Yvonne said enthusiastically. "And it would be so much fun if we could do some jumping together!" She paused, then added with a mischievous twinkle in her dark eyes, "Tor was impressed. You should have seen him watching you."

"What was there to be impressed about? I only did two jumps, and I messed up at first."

"It was the way you were riding the figures and cavaletti. You just looked so natural."

"I've been riding practically since I could walk!"

"I still think he likes you," Yvonne said.

"Well, I like him. What's the big deal?"

"It's more than that."

Samantha gave Yvonne a warning look. They'd

been through this before. Samantha couldn't seem to convince Yvonne that she and Tor were just friends and that she wasn't interested in dating anyone. With Pride's training schedule, she had more than enough to keep her busy, and she sure didn't want to turn into a boy-crazy airhead like a couple of girls in her class. But Samantha was thinking about how Tor had looked at her, too, and she felt a funny, pleasant tingle.

Yvonne grinned as if she were reading Samantha's thoughts.

"Come on," Samantha said abruptly to hide her embarrassment. "He's cooled out enough, and I still have to untack and brush him. My father will be picking us up in a little while."

When Samantha had finished with Cocoa, one of the stable grooms came to collect him and lead him back to his stall. Tor was busy getting horses ready for his class. Already a bunch of eight-, nine-, and ten-year-olds was gathering outside the stable office. "One of his beginner classes," Yvonne told Samantha.

As the girls were getting ready to leave, Tor came over to them. "Next week, same time," he told Samantha. "And the lessons are on me."

"But you can't—" Samantha began.

"I can do what I want with my own time," Tor said, smiling. "Look, I've got to go. See you in school tomorrow."

As soon as he was out of sight, Yvonne jabbed

Samantha with her elbow. "What did I tell you?" she said, chortling.

Samantha gave her friend a black look. "I don't even know if I'll take him up on it."

Yvonne grinned knowingly. "Yes, you will."

3

"HE WON IT, SAMMY!" ASHLEIGH SHOUTED OVER THE phone from Florida two and a half weeks later. "He was fantastic! He won by five lengths!"

"I saw," Samantha said excitedly. "We all watched it. How is he?" Samantha had been disappointed that she couldn't go to the Florida Derby in mid-March because of school, but Ashleigh and Charlie and Mike had gone with Pride.

"Just great, like he never ran a race. The reporters are mobbing us, and the Townsends are just about flipping out."

"The Townsends? You mean Brad is there?"

"Unfortunately," Ashleigh said. Samantha could almost picture the older girl wrinkling her nose. "And he's brought along a new girlfriend—Lavinia

Hotchkins-Ross. She's as much of a snob as he is. Brad brought her all over the stable and was talking as if *he'd* trained Pride. Well, he can brag all he wants, as long as he doesn't try interfering."

"He'd better not interfere," Samantha said.

"I think Pride misses you, Sammy," Ashleigh said. "He keeps looking over the stall door, like he's expecting you."

"I miss him, too. I wish I'd been there, but it didn't stop him from winning!"

"It sure didn't," Ashleigh said. "Anyway, we'll be home Monday. We decided not to try to drive straight through to Lexington. We're all too tired—except for Pride, that is." Ashleigh laughed.

"Congratulations, Ash!"

"Thanks, but we couldn't have done it without your help. See you Monday."

After Samantha hung up the phone in the kitchen, she went back into the living room, where her father, Yvonne, Mr. Reese, and Len were waiting.

"I guess Ashleigh's feeling on top of the world," her father said with a smile.

"She's pretty excited," Samantha said. "And so are the Townsends."

"Maybe now they'll stop hinting about bringing the colt back to Townsend Acres," said Len. "The colt feels at home here. He's happy."

"Did I hear you say Brad was at Gulfstream?" Yvonne asked.

"With a new girlfriend," Samantha said. "Her name is Lavinia Hotchkins-Ross, and Ashleigh says she's a snob."

Yvonne laughed. "In other words, she's just what Brad deserves."

"So I guess the next step is the Blue Grass," Mr. McLean said.

"And it's in Lexington, so I can be there!" Samantha said. "I just hope three big races before the Derby won't be too much for Pride," she added more somberly.

"The way he's come out of these last two races," her father said, "he shouldn't have any problems."

Samantha agreed, although she was still concerned about Pride's well-being. She glanced at the clock on the mantel. "Tor should be here in a minute. Do you mind if I show him around the farm?" she asked Mike's father.

"Of course not, this is your home, too," he said. "He's the fella who's giving you and Yvonne lessons and has his own Thoroughbred?"

Samantha and Yvonne both nodded.

"Hmmm," Mr. Reese said, "maybe we can sell him another." Then he laughed. "Don't worry. I'm not turning into a high-pressure salesman, and besides, Mike wants first grabs on anything we breed. I hear quite a few failed flat racers go on to become good jumpers, though."

"I've seen some of them at the stables," Yvonne said. "I'd love to have a chance to ride one, but most of them are all privately owned."

Samantha heard the sound of tires on gravel and went to the window to see Tor parking his small car near the barns. "Tor's here," she said. "I'll have him come in so I can introduce him to everyone."

"Hi," Tor said cheerfully when she opened the door. "I watched the race. I guess you're happy."

"Definitely!" Samantha said with a wide grin. "Come on in."

Tor followed her into the living room. Samantha made introductions, and the men rose to shake Tor's hand. "So I hear you have a Thoroughbred jumper," Mr. McLean said.

Tor described Top Hat and his history. "He's a great horse— all heart. He never did anything as a flat racer, but he can jump," he said proudly. "I really appreciate the chance to tour Whitebrook," he added to Mr. Reese.

"You're more than welcome here," Mr. Reese said. "Well, time to get back to work, I guess. I've got some pregnant mares I need to take a look at. Len, maybe you could give me a hand."

"Sure thing," the stable manager answered.

"Come on, Tor," Samantha said, "let's go for the grand tour."

Samantha and Yvonne led him outside, and

Samantha pointed across the drive. "There's the training oval. We can take a look at that first. It's a full mile. I know Mike worked hard to save enough money to put it in." They walked over to the white-railed oval, with its wide, well-harrowed dirt track. Beyond the inner rail, at its center, there was a smaller grass oval. "Mike trains both dirt and turf horses, so he needs both surfaces."

"So this is where you work Pride every morning," Tor said. "Do you work other horses, too?"

"Sometimes, when my father or Mike needs a hand. They only have one other regular rider, and he drives over every morning. It's not like Townsend Acres, where they have a half-dozen or more riders living on the grounds."

Next Samantha led him into the main stable building where the horses in training were housed. As they entered the dim interior, a sleek gray tiger cat with white markings jumped down from one of the stall barricades. Tail high, she trotted over to rub against Samantha's legs.

"Yours?" Tor asked, leaning down to pet the cat.

"No, Len's, but I love her. Actually, there are three of them. She's Snowshoe."

"Interesting name."

"Look at her feet," Samantha said. "Have you ever seen paws so big? There's also Jeeves, a huge black and white male, and their son, Sidney. Here they come." Samantha smiled as she watched a stocky, nearly all-black cat regally approach. He had four white socks and a strip of white under his chin that looked like a high-pointed collar.

Tor chuckled. "He looks like a butler."

"Len named him after a butler—Jeeves from the P. G. Wodehouse books."

Behind Jeeves, a mostly white half-grown kitten came bounding down the aisle. He made an arch-backed leap at Jeeves, and got hissed at and swatted for his trouble.

Yvonne reached down and picked up the kitten as he trotted up unfazed by his father's reprimand. A black band ran down Sidney's forehead, around his eyes, over his nose, and under his chin. "I just love his face! He looks like he's wearing a mask." Yvonne hugged the kitten and nuzzled her face in his fur. Sidney purred deeply, but was soon struggling to get down.

"Len says the cats are good company for the horses," Samantha explained.

"Yes, they are," Tor agreed. "Having another animal around keeps the horses from getting bored, and it seems to calm them. There are a couple at the riding stable, though they hide when the students are around."

"Sidney curls right up on Pride's back," Samantha said. "It's really funny to see, and Pride doesn't mind in the least. Well, come on, I guess

32

you want to see some of the horses."

Samantha led Tor and Yvonne down the aisle, describing the occupants of every stall. The cats followed along, sometimes jumping up on the stall doors. Mike had several two-year-olds that were being trained to race in the late spring or summer. Samantha's favorite was Sierra, a very dark chestnut, a son of Mike's stallion, Maxwell, and a Secretariat mare. Mike also had some three-year-olds of his own. One, Moondrone, hadn't shown much the previous year, but seemed to be coming into his own lately. There were a number of boarded horses that Mr. McLean trained for their owners, and Mike's five-year-old, Indigo, a big gray stallion. Mike had temporarily retired Indigo, but had put him back into training again. It paid off, because Indigo had improved with age and had won two graded stakes races in Florida over the winter.

They continued on to the much smaller stallion barn, where Mike's pride and joy, Jazzman, was stabled. The elegant black horse stuck his head over his stall door and whinnied a greeting.

"Hi, there, big guy," Samantha called. "I've brought you visitors." She stroked the stallion's sleek nose. "He was a big winner for Mike," she told Tor. "His first crop of foals is due this spring—actually one of them was born early this week, a colt, who looks just like him. I'll show him to you

33

when we go to the broodmare barn."

"He's a beauty," Tor said admiringly. "I can't help wondering how he'd do on a jump course."

"He's too valuable as a stud for that. Mike's had a lot of people interested in using him as a sire." Samantha gave the stallion a last pat, then led Tor and Yvonne on. "This bay is Maxwell. He never raced, but he has excellent bloodlines, and Mike bought him strictly for stud. His first crop of two-year-olds is in training, and my father's really impressed with a couple of them—a filly and a colt—Ms. Max, and Wellspring. I've ridden them both in workouts, and I think he's right. It'll be great for Mike if they do well, because he didn't have any big winners last year."

She showed Tor and Yvonne the last two stallions. "This chestnut is Russki, and the bay with the white blaze is Sadler's Station. Mike bought them at a dispersal this winter. Both of them raced in Europe and were brought to Kentucky for stud when they retired. Now, let's go see the mares. You've heard me talk about Fleet Goddess."

Tor chuckled. "Many times."

"Well, you'll get to see her."

"She's a beauty," Yvonne said. "Ashleigh retired her in the fall, and they're breeding her this spring to Jazzman. I can't wait to see *their* foal!"

They left the stallion barn and crossed over to the last barn in the complex. Several mares, heavy with foal, were out in the rapidly greening paddock, enjoying the grass and fresh air. In another paddock, yearlings were frolicking around. Fleet Goddess was in a separate paddock with two other mares who weren't in foal. She was big for a mare, and nearly black, with a white triangle on her forehead. She had won a fortune for Ashleigh. Samantha gave a sharp whistle, and the mare instantly lifted her head, then started cantering toward the paddock fence. She slid to a stop beside them and thrust her head over the fence to nudge Samantha affectionately.

"Hi, girl," Samantha said gently. "You out having a good time today? Sorry, I didn't bring any carrots." Goddess tossed her head and eyed Yvonne and Tor. "They don't have anything for you either," Samantha said with a laugh.

"Do you think she misses racing?" Tor asked. "I know Top Hat gets really antsy between show seasons."

"Actually, it's funny," Samantha said thoughtfully, "the other day when I was giving Pride a workout, I noticed Goddess standing at the corner of the paddock, just watching us. Maybe she does miss it, but she turned five in January, and Ashleigh didn't want to take the risk of racing her another year and possibly injuring her."

"Well, she'll make a good mother," Yvonne said.

"Let's hope. In the meantime, Ashleigh's told me I can take her out for rides around the farm to give her exercise and some excitement—nothing crazy, of course."

"That's pretty good of Ashleigh," Tor said, patting Goddess on the neck.

Samantha smiled and reached out to stroke Goddess. As she did, her fingers accidentally brushed against Tor's. Samantha quickly withdrew her hand, then immediately felt embarrassed by her reaction. She glanced over and saw that Tor was looking at her. She lowered her eyes, cleared her throat, and tried to remember what she had been about to say.

"Ah . . . yes, it is really good of Ashleigh, but she knows how close Goddess and I are, huh, girl?" Samantha spoke quickly, trying to recover her composure. What was the matter with her? she wondered. All they'd done was accidentally bump hands. She gave Goddess a parting kiss on her velvet nose, then turned away from the paddock fence. "The rest of the mares and young foals are inside," she said in a rush.

"So two foals were born since I was here last," Yvonne said excitedly. "I can't wait to see them!"

Samantha was relieved that Yvonne hadn't seemed to notice the uncomfortable moment. She was still trying to figure out why she had reacted so strangely to Tor's touch and didn't dare look at him. "They're cute," she said, "and there'll be more to come. There are a dozen mares in foal. Mike's father takes care of the breeding end of the farm. Mike and my father do all the training, with Charlie giving lots of advice. Charlie's sort of retired, but he'd get bored if he didn't get involved with the training, and he still helps train Pride."

Mares whickered as Samantha led the way down the aisle of the broodmare and yearling barn. Len and Mr. Reese were checking over one of the mares that was due to foal any day. "The two foals are down at the end," Len called out. "Figured you'd want a look at them."

Yvonne was the first to reach the two end stalls. She looked in eagerly over the half-door of the first and grinned at the fuzzy pale-brown foal within. "Aren't you a cutie!" she cried. "A little girl, too! Who's the sire?" she asked Samantha.

"Maxwell," Samantha answered. "Len's already nicknamed her Sadie. She's on the small side, but she's really perky." The tiny filly wobbled across the straw on too-long legs to get a better look at her visitors. Her dam, Virginia Belle, a light bay, whickered a warning. "It's okay, girl," Samantha said soothingly to the mare. "We won't bother her. We just want a look."

Sadie flicked her huge ears back and forth, made a high-pitched squeak, then took a playful leap across the straw. She looked back for their approval.

"She's showing off," Tor said with a smile. "When do they get to go out in the paddock?"

"Another week, maybe less, if the weather stays nice," Samantha answered. She was feeling more comfortable with Tor again, but she was very aware of Tor standing shoulder to shoulder with her.

They watched Sadie for a few more minutes, then moved to the opposite stall, where a coal-black foal was already standing alertly, ears pricked in the direction of their voices. "Jazzman's first foal," Samantha told Tor and Yvonne. "Like I said, he looks just like his father. His dam is a daughter of Secretariat, so he ought to be something special. She's also Sierra's dam."

"Secretariat, the Triple Crown winner?" Tor asked.

"And Horse of the Year two years running, among other things. Mike will have to wait a couple of years to see how this guy does, though. He'll have some foals of Maxwell to train in the meantime." Samantha paused. "I can't wait till they get back from Florida," she said with a sigh. "I miss Pride."

"I'll bet," Yvonne said. "But you'll be busy when he does get back—only a little over two weeks until the Blue Grass."

"I know—and by the way, I meant to tell you

38

that we have reserved seats for the Blue Grass, and I'd like both of you to come if you can."

"I wouldn't miss it!" Yvonne said instantly.

Tor flashed her a smile. "I'd love to come," he said, "but you're sure you have room? I've heard reserved seats for the Blue Grass are sold out way ahead of time."

"Positive," Samantha said. "And I'd like you to come. It's the least I can do for all the free lessons you've been giving me."

Tor laughed.

"Now, do you guys still want to go for a short ride?" Samantha said. "Mike said we can take out the exercise ponies. Of course, they're not actually ponies. Two are retired Thoroughbred geldings and the other is a mixed breed. We use them as pace horses and to help calm some of the high-strung young horses in training."

"Let's go," Yvonne and Tor said in one breath.

4

SAMANTHA OPENED THE *LEXINGTON HERALD* SPORTS pages the morning after the Blue Grass and saw the blaring headlines. "Pride Romps Home! A Sure Derby Favorite!" The cover story glowingly described Pride's performance in beating more of the top three-year-old colts in the country. "There seems no question the racing world is witnessing a rising star and maybe the next Triple Crown champion," Samantha read.

She looked up as her father entered the kitchen and poured himself a cup of coffee. He smiled. "Reading about the race?"

Samantha nodded as she took a bite of her cereal.

"Pretty heady stuff," he said.

"Incredible, but it almost makes me nervous. They're talking about him being the favorite for the Derby, and the Derby is only three weeks away!"

"I know what you mean, but I wouldn't get nervous yet. He came out of the race very well. Give him a few days' rest and just enough work to keep him on his toes."

"Ashleigh, Charlie, and I were talking about his training schedule last night. I won't start working him until the end of the week, and then only do some slow gallops."

The phone rang, and her father picked it up.

"For you, Sammy," he said.

She got up and took the phone. "Hi, Ash. I was just reading the write-ups about the race. She did? When? Oh, my gosh! A filly? Is Wonder all right?" Samantha turned her head to look at her father. "Dad! Wonder's had her foal—this morning—a filly!" She put her mouth back to the receiver. "Can we come over? Have you told Mike? Okay—great! We'll be there!"

Her father was smiling when she hung up. "I take it everything's all right."

"Yes! Ashleigh was there the whole time. Wonder didn't have any problems, and her filly is gorgeous, Ashleigh said. Mike's driving over in a few minutes, and he'll give us a ride."

"Better get these dishes cleaned up, then." Mr.

McLean drained his coffee cup while Samantha took her cereal bowl to the sink and washed it. She had already been out to the stable to feed Pride before she'd come in to breakfast. Mike was waiting by his pickup as Samantha and her father left the cottage and headed down the path to the drive.

"Some kind of a weekend!" Mike said with a grin. "Pride wins the Blue Grass, and his half sister is born the next day. Not bad!"

"A good-luck omen," Mr. McLean said.

They traveled the distance to the Griffen farm in record time. Ashleigh was waiting outside the foaling barn, her face wreathed in a smile.

"Come on," she called as soon as they were out of the car. "My mom and dad are with her. Wait till you see the foal. She's beautiful—and she looks like Wonder and Pride—a neat little chestnut!" Ashleigh hurried into the barn. "Mr. Townsend's on his way."

Ashleigh's parents were standing outside Wonder's huge box stall. They waved and smiled as the others hurried up. Samantha eagerly looked over the stall door. Wonder was standing near the back of her stall, looking very pleased with herself. Her little filly, only a few hours old, was already up on her feet, nursing. Wonder nickered, and her foal, who had had her fill, lifted her head to stare curiously at the new visitors. Her oversize ears flopped back and forth, and she swished her brush of a tail.

"How cute!" Samantha said. "She looks just like Pride . . . only not as big."

"You can go in and say hello," Ashleigh told her. "Wonder won't mind."

Samantha quickly unlatched the stall door and went in. The foal took a nervous, wobbly step backward, but Samantha went to Wonder first. "Congratulations, girl!" she said, hugging the mare's neck. "Your foal is just perfect, and your son won a very big race yesterday, too."

Wonder bobbed her head as if she understood, then blew softly into Samantha's hand. "I'm just going to say hello to her," Samantha added, turning toward the foal. By now the tiny filly had gotten over her initial nervousness, and she took a curious, tentative step toward Samantha. Samantha knelt down on the bedding and gently ran a hand down the foal's fuzzy copper-colored back. "Aren't you something?" she said with a sigh. "What are you going to call her?" she asked Ashleigh.

Ashleigh laughed. "I haven't thought that far ahead, though she looks like a little princess to me . . . Wonder's Princess? Princess Wonder? Her sire is Baldasar. Her grandsire is Townsend Pride, but we already have a Pride."

"Townsend Princess, I think," a voice said from outside the stall.

"Mr. Townsend!" Ashleigh said. "Come and have a look at her."

The foal's half-owner said hello to the Griffens, Mr. McLean, and Mike. Then he stepped inside the stall to look the foal over. A moment later he nodded and smiled. "Healthy and alert," he said, "though in a way, I was hoping for a colt. A colt would have more value at stud, but if she performs like her dam, we won't have anything to worry about."

Why did the Townsends always seem to think of everything in terms of money? Samantha wondered. The filly was gorgeous.

"And I think Townsend Princess would be an appropriate name," he continued with a smile, "especially considering that we lost Townsend Prince last year."

Samantha noticed Ashleigh's thoughtful expression. She guessed that the older girl would have preferred choosing a name herself, but Townsend Prince was Wonder's halfbrother and had been a champion racehorse and valuable stud until, after a freak accident the year before, he'd had to be put down.

"Well, this has definitely been a good weekend," he said as he left the stall. "Quite a difference from last year at this time."

Samantha had to agree with that. Last year, Clay Townsend had been on the verge of selling his interest in Wonder and Pride.

"You know what to do," Charlie told Samantha two weeks later as she prepared to ride Pride out for his workout. "You've got a way with him. You don't need much advice from me."

Samantha stared at the old trainer for a second, a flush rising up in her cheeks. Charlie was stingy with his praise, which made it all the more important. Before she could say anything, he pulled down the brim of his hat and started walking toward the training-oval rail.

Samantha had noticed that he and Ashleigh had recently been giving her more and more responsibility in Pride's training. Ashleigh trusted her with the colt, and since the older girl couldn't get to Whitebrook all the time, she needed help from Samantha, who had learned so much about training in the last year. Samantha loved every minute of it, so it didn't seem like work, and Pride deserved most of the credit. He was always so willing and eager—and smart.

With a smile on her face, Samantha heeled Pride forward through the gap onto the track. Yvonne was already standing at the rail. Since it was a weekend, she had spent the night at

Samantha's. They'd spent quite a bit of time together during their spring vacation the previous week, and Samanatha had managed to squeeze in a couple of jumping lessons with Tor. His praise at her improvement pleased and encouraged her, but her thoughts were consumed by the exciting prospect of Pride running in the Kentucky Derby. At times Samantha felt like pinching herself to be sure she wasn't dreaming it all!

"Okay Pride," she said to the beautiful colt. "This will be your last big workout before you go to Churchill Downs. Let's do it right."

Pride huffed out an excited breath and arched his neck as Samantha urged him into a trot. He set out with brisk, springy strides and eagerly kicked into a faster pace when Samantha signaled him to canter.

For the last week she'd been working him easily—long, slow gallops, with only a few short breezes. He was already in prime fitness, and the object was to keep the colt at that peak without putting unnecessary stress on him. Today, though, he needed a good half-mile breeze to sharpen him up. Ashleigh would give him a couple of workouts on the Churchill Downs track, but the main purpose of those works would be to familiarize Pride with the track and the surface.

Samantha lapped the track once, then readied herself as they approached the milepost, crouching lower in the saddle. "Ready, boy?" she murmured, but there was no question of that. As soon as she gave Pride rein, he was gone. She kept him to a slow gallop through the first half-mile. Coming down the backstretch, she watched for the half-mile pole and prepared. They swept up to it, and she gave Pride more rein. "Go!" she cried.

He surged forward eagerly, lengthening his stride and picking up his pace. They were flying now, and Samantha nearly laughed aloud at the thrill of their speed, the wind whipping in her face, the power of the magnificent animal beneath her. Around the far turn they pounded. Pride seemed to have wings on his feet, so effortlessly did his strides eat up the distance. Off the far turn and into the stretch, Samantha barely had to ask the big colt to change leads. He switched easily from his left to his right lead, giving him an extra burst of strength for the last eighth-mile. They roared through the last furlong and swept past the milepost. She didn't need a stopwatch to tell her their time was good.

Samantha stood in the stirrups, one hand gripping the reins, the other firmly patting Pride's neck. He dropped back to a canter, tossing his head, exhilarated.

"That's the way, big boy!" Samantha cried proudly. What a workout! Pride had done everything perfectly. Now, if he could repeat that kind of effort in the Kentucky Derby, she knew he'd win—she just knew it!

Yvonne hurried over as Samantha rode Pride off the track. Mr. McLean, Mike, and Mr. Reese had come to watch the end of the workout, and from a distance, Samantha's father gave her the high sign.

"He did the last half in forty-four and change, the last quarter in twenty-two flat," Charlie said, pushing back his hat.

Samantha reined Pride to a stop in front of the old trainer. "Incredible!" she cried. "I knew it. I could feel it! I guess he's set."

"Yup," Charlie answered, "if nothing goes wrong between now and next Saturday. We'll van him over Monday." He ran his hands over Pride's legs and gave the colt a careful scrutiny.

"Too bad Ashleigh didn't get to see this morning's workout," Samantha said. "What a rotten time to get the flu. I know she would have been as excited as I am!"

"You bet she would have," Mike put in. "Anyway, it sounds like one of those twenty-four-hour things. I think she wore herself out studying for last week's finals. She should be fine tomorrow, so she can head over to Louisville with Pride."

"I hope so. I just wish I could go, too," Samantha said as she dismounted and pulled up the stirrups, "but there's no way I can go to Louisville when I have school."

"At least you'll get to take Friday off," Yvonne told her, "and Charlie and Ashleigh will be with Pride."

Samantha nodded, but she knew she would miss the colt during those last tense days leading up to the Derby. She wondered how she'd ever be able to concentrate in her classes. Thankfully her father had agreed to let her take Friday off. Her grades were good, he knew how she felt about being with Pride, and he agreed with Samantha that participating firsthand in the most famous of American horse races was an education in itself, particularly when she was planning on a career in racing.

"I'd better get you cooled out," she said to the colt. Her father and Mike still had horses to work, but Mike would be doing the riding that morning with the help of his one hired rider, Sheldon White. Samantha had the rest of the morning to dote on Pride. Charlie gave Samantha a nod, and she and Yvonne led Pride off to the barn where she untacked him and covered him with a light sheet.

"I can't get over how good he looked," Yvonne said as they walked along the grassy area around the barns. "Sammy, he's just amazing. I wish someone had taken a video of the workout so you could see."

Samantha smiled. "I can feel it when we have a good workout, but I wouldn't mind seeing it on film, too," she said. "I'm getting so excited about the Derby. I keep telling myself not to get too hyper—but Pride racing in the Derby! A horse I helped train—it's just such an amazing feeling."

"You don't have to tell me," Yvonne said, pushing her straight dark hair away from her face. "Oh, did you finish your article for Maureen?"

Samantha nodded. "I gave it to her before vacation. She called me last week to say she loved it. She wants the next one to be a recap of the Derby. I just hope the race turns out the way I want, so I can do some bragging about Pride." She laughed. "But I do that all the time, anyway."

"Well, so would I if I had a horse like him!" Yvonne said. "Going to the Derby with you will be so incredible. And Tor's excited, too."

"He's been so great about giving me free lessons, and I think he's getting interested in racing."

"That's the only reason you asked him?" Yvonne teased.

"Well, no," Samantha admitted, turning her head so Yvonne couldn't see her blush. "He's fun to be with. . . . But we're just good friends," she added defensively.

51

Yvonne kept grinning. "Yup."

"All right," Samantha admitted, "I think he's really cute and really nice. I like him a lot, and we both love horses. But I'm not sure how I feel otherwise. Sometimes I feel really strange around him, but right now, the most important thing is Pride and the Derby. I can't think about anything else."

5

SAMANTHA GRIPPED HER BINOCULARS AND KEPT THEM trained on Pride as the field for the Kentucky Derby warmed up. Next to her, Yvonne was chewing a fingernail and Tor had his program rolled in a tight wad. The noisy crowds in the packed grandstand had hushed a little as they, too, studied the field. Mr. McLean turned around in his seat one row down where he sat with Charlie and Mike. "He looks cool as a cucumber," he said to Samantha.

Samantha nodded. Her throat felt so tight with anticipation, she didn't trust her voice. Pride did look calm and confident. He pranced beneath Ashleigh with head and tail high, and he wasn't showing any of the nerves some of the other colts

53

in the field were displaying. He didn't fidget, and there wasn't a sign of sweat on his brilliant copper coat.

Ashleigh had said Pride had gone well in his two light workouts earlier in the week, but he'd certainly been overjoyed to see Samantha when she'd arrived at Churchill Downs on Friday morning with her father. She had lavished attention on him, while Ashleigh, Charlie, and her father had kept the curious away from his stall. Earlier that afternoon, she'd given him a good grooming, so that now his copper coat glistened in the sun, and his mane and tail flowed like silk. Moments before, she had led him proudly around the walking ring, aware of the admiring gazes from the crowd. And now he was out on the track, preparing to run the biggest race of his life.

"Ultrasound looks awfully good, too, and that gray, Count Abdul . . ." Yvonne said worriedly.

Samantha had been studying Ultrasound, a light bay colt who'd lost to Pride the previous year. His breeding was as good or better than Pride's, since his sire was Seattle Slew, the 1977 Triple Crown winner. Although he'd had a late start in his three-year-old season, he'd won every race he'd been in since. The roan, Count Abdul, was a late bloomer, who had suddenly started making a name for himself on the West Coast tracks that winter. But he'd never raced in the East, so

Samantha wasn't sure how he'd perform. The odd-smakers weren't sure either. He was going off at 8 to 1. Pride was the favorite at 5 to 2, with Ultrasound just behind him at 3 to 1. But Samantha knew there could still be surprises in the rest of the field. Even though Pride had beaten several of them in the Blue Grass, these horses were the best three-year-olds in the country, with one horse from Canada and another from England.

Pride had drawn post position five—not the best, but not the worst either, in the twelve-horse field. "If he makes a clean break, he should be fine," Samantha said, watching intently as Ashleigh and Pride waited to load into the gate. Unlike several of the other colts, who balked and had to be pushed into the gate, Pride behaved like a gentleman. His mind was already on business as he walked forward without hesitation.

As Ashleigh settled in the saddle, she took a firm grip on the reins and wrapped her fingers tightly in Pride's long mane. Samantha knew Ashleigh would need that extra grip if she was to stay aboard when Pride surged out of the gate. Ultrasound had drawn the eighth post position, but since he had developed into a late closer, his position at the start of the mile-and-a-quarter race wasn't as important. Count Abdul, who'd acted up while being loaded, was in the third slot.

Then bells rang, and the gate doors snapped

open. "They're off for the running of the Kentucky Derby!" shouted the announcer.

Samantha hunched forward in her seat. "A good break," she said as the field swept up past the grandstand for the first time. Pride had jumped out to an early lead, but two horses rushed up behind him as Ashleigh moved him in closer to the rail. Then Count Abdul moved into third on the outside, a perfect position to make a later move. Samantha knew it wasn't going to be an easy race for Pride—the run for the roses never was. Every horse owner and jockey in the field wanted *his* horse to go down in the record books as the winner of the Kentucky Derby.

Samantha was silent as the field, led by Pride, moved into the clubhouse turn. Ashleigh had the big colt settled in nicely. The fractions weren't too fast, which would help Pride at the end of the race when the colt's biggest challenge would come. But Samantha didn't breathe easily for long. Count Abdul started moving up on Pride's flank.

Samantha groaned. "Oh, no. He's going to press the pace. The last thing we need is a speed duel!" She heard Charlie's angry mutter from the row ahead as Count Abdul continued gaining on Pride. Samantha saw Ashleigh glance back quickly under her arm, but she held Pride steady. The colt did not like running behind other horses, though, and it would be almost impossible for

Ashleigh to hold him once he saw the other horse gaining on him.

And now Pride had seen Count Abdul. Samantha saw Ashleigh straining to hold him as he tried to increase his speed. He held Count Abdul off by a neck and would have increased the gap between them more if Ashleigh had let him have his way.

Samantha saw the fractions for the half-mile and groaned again. Pride had done the first quarter-mile in twenty-four seconds, a fairly moderate pace, but he'd just ticked off the half in forty-five seconds. "Too fast," Samantha cried.

"But he's keeping the lead," Tor said softly.

"He'll burn himself out. He won't have anything left. And the early speed sets the race up perfectly for Ultrasound. The leaders will be tiring, and he'll fly past them at the wire."

"An unexpected speed duel!" the announcer was shouting. "The West Coast invader is pressing Wonder's Pride. The big chestnut colt isn't giving an inch, despite Ashleigh Griffen's efforts to hold him. They have seven lengths on the field as they come down the backstretch. And now Ultrasound is finding his best stride. He's moving up through horses. It's Wonder's Pride, Count Abdul, Ricky's Charmer, Knightshade, Ultrasound moving like a bullet! The rest are far back."

"Suicidal!" Charlie growled. "Darn jock knows he's not going to win the race. He's playing spoiler, trying to burn Pride out, making him put out too much too soon."

Samantha was thinking the same thing as Pride and Count Abdul swept into the far turn. Pride still hadn't given an inch, but the fractions were too, too fast. Even if Pride held out to win, he'd come out of the race exhausted.

"And they're into the turn!" came the announcer's increasingly excited voice. "Wonder's Pride, Count Abdul, neck and neck! Ultrasound now up into third and closing fast. He only has three lengths to make up. Can Wonder's Pride hold out?"

Samantha had only one small hope. She saw Pride change leads for the stretch drive, but she could also see that Ashleigh still hadn't given him full rein. Her hands, gripping the reins, were well back on Pride's neck. Ashleigh would know how much horse she still had under her. Did she think Pride could come up with another gear?

Samantha was barely breathing as Pride and Count Abdul approached the eighth pole. "The mile in a minute thirty-five!" the announcer screeched. Samantha swallowed. Fast—very, very fast. Then she saw Ashleigh make her move. Her hands slid up Pride's neck, letting him out. Ultrasound was within easy striking distance on the outside of Count Abdul and losing no momentum.

"Go!" she screamed at the top of her lungs. "Go, Pride! Come on, baby!"

They'd all risen in their seats. Yvonne was jumping up and down in place. Tor was hoarsely shouting his encouragement. Charlie's hat was crushed in his hands.

And Pride did have another gear. The instant Ashleigh gave him rein, he extended his stride and shot forward. Within four strides, he'd left Count Abdul eating dust, but Ultrasound was still roaring up the middle of the track.

"Wonder's Pride has something left," cried the announcer. "After that punishing speed duel, he's found another gear—and Ultrasound isn't going to catch him this time! What a race! An amazing performance! Wonder's Pride *wins* it by two lengths, then Ultrasound, Count Abdul holding on for third. And the big chestnut has taken two-fifths of a second off the track record!"

Samantha was shaking. She couldn't seem to stop. Yvonne squeezed her friend's shoulders. "Wow!" she said, beaming.

Tor gave Samantha an impulsive hug. His face was alight. "I've never seen anything like it."

"I'm so happy," Samantha said with a gasp. "I always believed in him, but it was better than anything I ever dreamed!" There were tears of happiness in her eyes, and she tried to dash them away with the back of her hand. "Oh, my gosh, we have to go to the winner's circle, don't we? I'll be leading Pride in."

"We sure do," her father said with a broad grin.

"I hope he's come out of it all right," Samantha said breathlessly. "It was such a hard race."

"He looks okay coming back down the track," Charlie said. His blue eyes were twinkling as he shook out and replaced his hat. "Too soon to tell, though."

They pushed through the crowd and made their way down the grandstand steps. The noise was almost deafening. Tor, Mike, and Mr. McLean helped clear a path, and moments later they were approaching the winner's circle as Ashleigh proudly rode Pride off the track. She was grinning ear-to-ear, but Samantha was focused on Pride. His chestnut coat was darkened from the sweat of his efforts, but his head was high and his step springy as Samantha rushed over. She took Pride's lead shank from the pocket of her green and gold Townsend Acres jacket and clipped it to Pride's bridle. As excited as the colt was, he still turned his head to affectionately lip Samantha's red hair.

"I love you, big guy. You were incredible," Samantha praised, taking the colt's head and kissing his nose. Then she looked up at Ashleigh. "What a race—just unbelievable!"

"I know," Ashleigh said with a happy sigh. "I tried to sit cool through that speed duel, but it wasn't easy. He fought me every inch of the way. But he had something left!" Ashleigh patted Pride's neck, and they walked into the winner's circle. Samantha was so dazed by Pride's victory that she barely noticed the sea of people and cameras. Then, as Samantha held Pride, Ashleigh dismounted and removed her saddle so that she could weigh in.

The colt blew hot breaths against Samantha's hand, and his sides heaved from his exertions, but otherwise he seemed fine as he pricked his ears and studied the crowd around him.

Others had come into the ring—track dignitaries, a television crew and announcer, and the Townsends, Clay, Brad, and a beautifully dressed young woman. She had her arm through Brad's, and her shoulder-length blond hair shimmered in the sunlight. Ashleigh returned to remount as the luxuriant blanket of red roses was draped over Pride's shoulders.

The Townsends walked over. Mr. Townsend gave Samantha a quick smile, then took Pride's lead shank from her hand. "I'll hold him for the photos," he said. Brad and Lavinia immediately crowded in next to Mr. Townsend at Pride's head, stepping right in front of Samantha. They smiled broadly for the cameras as if *they'd* had something to do with Pride's victory.

Ashleigh gave Samantha a startled and unhappy

look when she saw that Samantha had been shoved out of the picture. But she turned away as the television cameras started to roll.

Samantha stood silently a few feet away, the heat rising in her cheeks. She supposed she'd just been shown her place as Pride's lowly groom. But she had more of a bond to Pride than either of the Townsends!

Charlie came up beside her. "Afraid this is what you're going to have to expect from here on out. The Townsends are going to want all the glory."

"But Brad's girlfriend?" she muttered with quiet anger.

"I agree, but that's life, Sammy. It won't do any good to show how angry you are."

"I wasn't going to," Samantha answered, but her face was set as Ashleigh dismounted again. And her blood really boiled when she overheard Brad say to Lavinia, "I always knew this guy was going to be great." How can he have the nerve to say that? Samantha thought. Brad had wanted to sell Pride!

Mr. Townsend didn't even glance at Samantha as he casually handed her back Pride's reins and stepped across to join Ashleigh and the track officials for the presentation of the trophy and the car that Ashleigh had won as winning jockey.

Charlie handed Samantha Pride's green and gold satin sheet and went to unsaddle the colt. As he removed Pride's saddle, Samantha quickly went to work covering Pride in his satin sheet. He nickered to her and rubbed his head affectionately against her arm. "You did a wonderful job," she praised. "I'm so proud of you! Let's get you back to the barn and cool you out. Then I've got a special treat for your dinner."

With her father, Charlie, Yvonne, and Tor walking beside her, Samantha led the magnificent colt out of the winner's circle and toward the barn area. As they passed the grandstands, eager fans in the crowd took photos. Pride tossed his head for them, as if he knew he was the star. "The next Triple Crown winner!" someone called enthusiastically. Samantha grinned and patted Pride's neck, forgetting for the moment her anger about the scene in the winner's circle.

After Charlie had checked Pride over, Samantha sponged the colt down and started walking him. Mr. McLean and Charlie shooed all the reporters away. "Give the colt a break," Charlie told them gruffly. "He's had enough excitement for one day."

"I've never seen anything like it," Tor said with a laugh as they headed down between the shedrows. "Total madness, but he definitely deserves the attention."

"Ashleigh told me what it would be like if he won," Samantha answered. "She went through it all with Wonder. But I'm still amazed."

"And it's only going to get worse," Yvonne said. "You heard what they were calling from the crowd. They think Pride's going to be the next Triple Crown winner."

Samantha heaved a happy sigh. "I haven't let myself think that far ahead. I'm almost afraid to."

"But I have a feeling Pride could do it," Tor said quietly.

Samantha glanced up and saw that his blue eyes were riveted on her face.

His intent gaze gave her a strange tingly feeling, and she looked away in confusion. "As Charlie would say, a lot of things could happen between now and then," she said softly.

"And as my father always tells me before I ride into the show ring," Tor answered, "think positively."

"I tell her that all the time," Yvonne said with a chuckle. "But it's hard to make her listen."

A halfhour later, when they returned Pride to his stall, the backside had quieted down a little. Ashleigh had arrived at the stall after showering and changing out of her silks. She immediately ran over and hugged Samantha.

"We did it!" she cried. "I still haven't calmed down. Pride won the Derby!"

"Now I know how you felt when Wonder won," Samantha answered, returning Ashleigh's hug.

"It's something, isn't it?" Ashleigh said. "How is he?"

"Great. Charlie's checked him over. He's all cooled out and cleaned up. I gave him a special mash, and he dug right into it."

"Good," Ashleigh said with relief. "It was such a tough race, I was worried he'd come out of it exhausted. Sammy, I'm sorry about what happened in the winner's circle. It wasn't fair for you to be pushed out of the picture. If it wasn't for your help, Pride might not even be here right now. And for Brad's girlfriend to be in the photo . . . it makes me absolutely sick!"

Samantha smiled sourly. "You're not the only one. But it's okay. I was pretty angry, but I'm all right now."

"I've made sure the reporters know how big a part you've played in Pride's training," Ashleigh said. "I'm not going to let the Townsends try to take the credit."

"Thanks, Ash, but all that really matters is that Pride keep running well."

Ashleigh scowled, then her face brightened. "I have something for you, Sammy. I was going to give it to you before the race, but things were too crazy." For her interviews after the race, Ashleigh had changed into a tailored blue suit and silk blouse. She looked very pretty and professional. She reached into her jacket pocket and withdrew an envelope, which she handed to Samantha. "This is to say thanks for all you've done for me and

65

Pride—call it a bonus if you want."

Samantha's eyes widened when she pulled out a check for five thousand dollars. She gasped, blinked, and looked at the figure again, and her jaw fell open. "But you already pay me for grooming and riding Pride . . . and I love doing it anyway."

"I *wanted* to do it, Sammy. You deserve it. You've been so wonderful with Pride. I couldn't have done it by myself."

"But it's so much!" Samantha cried.

"Do you know how much Pride won today?" Ashleigh asked with a smile. "Put it toward college if you want, though knowing you, you'll probably win a ton of scholarships."

The two girls hugged again, and Samantha felt the sting of tears in her eyes. "Thank you, Ash . . . thanks so much!"

"Thank *you*! Now, everyone get cleaned up. We're going out to celebrate. That means you, too, Charlie." Ashleigh laughed at the old trainer's disgruntled expression.

"You know I hate all that fancy stuff. The Townsends coming, too?"

"Nope. They're celebrating with their own friends, not that I mind. I was invited to one of the big parties, too, but I didn't want to go."

"In that case, guess I could come with you," Charlie said.

Soon they were all leaving the backside for dinner in Louisville. Samantha had checked Pride over one last time, but she knew he would be in good hands with the tight security on the backside.

She was still reeling from Ashleigh's generous gift and Pride's incredible performance. "This has been some kind of day!" she murmured.

"You can say that again," Tor agreed. "Now I guess it's on to the Preakness and Belmont."

"Yes," Samantha said, sighing, "but I've got to get through this day first." Then she laughed. "Wow! Will I ever be able to write a great article for the school paper!"

6

MONDAY MORNING AT SCHOOL, SAMANTHA WAS MOBBED by classmates congratulating her on the Derby. "We saw you on TV!" a girl in her English class cried. "What a beautiful horse!" another said. "So he's the one you've been writing about. What was it like?" said a third.

Samantha tried to answer the flood of questions.

"I was there, too," Yvonne exclaimed. "It was incredible!"

Maureen came shouldering in through the crowd, eyes alight behind her glasses. "So how soon do you think you can get an article done? Or are you going to wait and write about the Preakness, too?"

"Gosh, Maureen," Yvonne exclaimed, "give her

a break! The paper doesn't come out for weeks!"

"Yeah, I know, but they've made me features editor." Maureen shrugged sheepishly. "I guess I get carried away."

Samantha laughed. "No kidding, but don't worry, I'll get an article done soon. I've already started. I was too excited to sleep the night before the Derby, so I started to write then."

"We decided at the newspaper meeting you missed to have a special graduation issue in mid-June," Maureen said. "So maybe I can get something in that, but I know there'll be a lot of articles about graduation and the prom, summer jobs and stuff. We'll see. So did you see any famous people?" Maureen went on excitedly.

"Lots!" Samantha said, laughing. She rattled off names of movie stars and other celebrities, and Yvonne added a name or two. "Right," Samantha said. "I was so busy with Pride I didn't get to see as much of the crowd as Yvonne did."

"Hey, we'd better get a move on or we'll be late to homeroom," Yvonne said.

The crowd quickly dispersed as the warning bell rang, but Samantha heard the same questions all day long. Juniors and seniors she barely knew came up and congratulated her. At lunch Tor sat with Samantha and Yvonne.

"How's it feel being a celebrity?" he asked teasingly.

"Pride's the star, not me," Samantha answered, then grinned. "But it's neat. You'll be a celebrity, too, when you and Top Hat start winning blue ribbons in the big shows this summer."

"Unfortunately, people don't pay as much attention to show jumping as they do racing."

"And if you ask me," Yvonne said, "jumping takes a lot more skill."

"I think it does, too," Samantha agreed. "Until I started learning to jump, I didn't realize how much skill."

"Speaking of lessons," Tor said, "I don't suppose you'll have time for one this week or next."

"With two weeks to the Preakness, I'm going to be pretty busy with Pride," Samantha said with disappointment.

"You can take one hour off after school," Yvonne said firmly.

"Well, all right, I'll try." Samantha was enjoying the lessons, and having Tor as her instructor made them even better, she realized. She glanced over at him and saw him smiling at her.

"Don't worry," he said. "We all know what's most important to you right now. After the Triple Crown, I'll give you some extra lessons. How does that sound?"

Samantha returned his smile. "I'd like that."

*   *   *

71

When Samantha arrived home from school that afternoon, she saw Ashleigh's shining new Chrysler parked in the drive. Samantha knew how thrilled Ashleigh had been to get the car as the winning jockey of the Kentucky Derby. Her old one wasn't that dependable anymore, though Ashleigh's brother, Rory, had already claimed the secondhand sedan for when he got his license in a year.

Samantha hurried into the house to change. She hadn't worked Pride that morning, since he needed a few days off after his efforts in the Derby, but she planned on taking him out for a long walk that afternoon.

Snowshoe and Sidney came scurrying down the aisle toward her as she entered the barn and tagged at her heels as she went over to Pride's stall. Ashleigh and Mike were standing in the aisle outside the colt's stall, talking and looking very serious.

"Things are never boring," Ashleigh said when Samantha joined them. "I had a real interesting phone call this afternoon."

Samantha frowned. Her first thought was that the Townsends wanted Wonder and her foal or Pride back at Townsend Acres, and her stomach tightened.

"I got an offer on my interest in Pride," Ashleigh said.

"You did?" Samantha gasped. "Who from?"

"An agent for one of the Maktoums. You know who they are."

Samantha nodded, stunned. The extraordinarily wealthy Arabs were very active in racing, and they owned stud farms and stables all over the world. "How much?" she asked tightly.

"Two million."

"What! But—but that's only for half interest!"

"They're comparing him to the next Secretariat," Mike said. "Two million isn't out of line. In fact, if he goes on to win the Preakness and Belmont, or even just one of them, he'll have earned nearly that much in one year."

Samantha felt the ground lurch beneath her. "You aren't selling, are you?"

Suddenly Ashleigh laughed. "If you could see your face, Sammy . . . No, of course, I'm not selling! Absolutely not—even if they offered twice that much." Her jaw tightened. "Mike and I made a couple of phone calls to people we know. The rumor is that the Townsends and the Maktoums are buddy-buddy."

"I can't believe Mr. Townsend would try to get someone to buy you out," Samantha said.

"No—I don't think he's behind it, but I wouldn't be surprised if he knew about it and he and Maktoum have already talked. Anyway, I turned them down."

"I don't think that's the end of it, though," Mike said. "This probably won't be the only offer Ashleigh gets. I hate to say it, but a lot of big shots look at Ashleigh and think, 'Eh, she's just a kid. What does she know? She's not likely to refuse an even moderately decent offer.'" Mike smiled. "Of course, that just shows how little they know about Ashleigh."

Ashleigh and Mike exchanged a look, and Samantha smiled, slowly letting out a breath of relief. "I was planning on taking Pride out for a walk."

"I figured you would," Ashleigh said. "I was just in checking him over. It's amazing how well he's come out of the race. Huh, boy?"

Pride stuck his head over the door and whickered. He knew what Samantha's appearance meant, and he was eager to get out of his stall.

"Yes, we'll go out for a nice long walk, Pride," Samantha said.

"I'll go with you," Ashleigh told her. "I want to take Goddess out for a treat, now that she's an expectant mom."

Samantha remembered how thrilled they had all been when the vet had confirmed that Fleet Goddess was in foal to Jazzman.

"Any foal of Jazzman and Fleet Goddess is going to be a beauty," Mike said, grinning. "I can't wait until his first foals go into training."

74

"Well, you have Maxwell's two-year-olds to train for now," Samantha pointed out. "Are you still bringing Ms. Max and Wellspring up to Belmont for their maiden races next month?" Although Samantha had ridden both young horses in workouts, her father and Mike, and their daily rider, Sheldon White, did most of their training work.

Mike nodded. "It should work out well with Pride going up to Belmont. We can take all of them up together. I was hoping Sierra would be ready, too, but he's not."

"Do you think he's going to be a late bloomer?" Samantha asked.

"I don't know. He's really grown into himself nicely. He's got beautiful confirmation and movement, but he can be a handful. He's definitely got a mind of his own and loves to pull fast ones on Sheldon when they're working. I've tried taking him out myself, and it's almost like he's testing his rider. He doesn't settle. His mind sure isn't on running."

"He'll settle down eventually," Samantha said. "Maybe I could take him out one morning."

"Right!" Ashleigh agreed with a laugh. "Maybe he needs a feminine touch."

Mike gave her a look, then shrugged. "Maybe he does. I'm getting to the point where I'll try anything. Sure, try him out tomorrow if you want, Sammy."

"Great. I'll have plenty of time, since Pride won't be working until the end of the week." As she spoke, she unlatched Pride's door. He was growing very impatient, huffing and stomping.

"All right, Pride," Samantha soothed. "We're going out. Just let me clip on your lead shank."

"I'll go get Goddess," Ashleigh said. "And I'll meet you out by the pasture."

As Ashleigh walked away, Mike headed off, too. "I've got work to do," he said. "See you later."

Samantha, Pride, Ashleigh, and Goddess had a nice walk, circling behind the white-fenced paddocks of Whitebrook, over the mowed grass lanes separating them, and onto a cleared trail through the small woodland behind. Awkward foals scampered in one paddock with their dams, and in another paddock, a half-dozen yearlings galloped about in play. The air was lush with spring scents.

"How's Princess?" Samantha asked. She'd only seen Wonder's new foal once more since she'd been born. There just hadn't been time to get over to the Griffens' farm.

"Growing by leaps and bounds," Ashleigh answered. "She's even pushing some of the bigger foals around. She sure lives up to her name and definitely thinks she's special."

"You've decided to go along with Mr. Townsend and call her Townsend Princess?" Samantha asked.

Ashleigh shrugged. "With everything else going on, I didn't have the energy to argue, and it's not a bad name."

"No, it's not a bad name at all," Samantha agreed.

"And I don't want to start an argument that might get Mr. Townsend thinking about moving them back to Townsend Acres."

"Hank's told Charlie that things are still pretty tight over there," Samantha said, "though the new breeding manager's supposed to be good."

"I've heard they only have about half as many horses in training as they used to," Ashleigh said. "But Pride's winnings should spark some interest in their stallions and new foals, which could generate more income—if Brad doesn't go out and blow the money on some worthless horses like he did before."

"At least I don't have to be living on the same farm as Brad anymore," Samantha said.

"No. Whitebrook's a much nicer place to be, and I know Mike's really happy that he offered your father the job. Your dad's a good trainer."

Samantha smiled. "I know."

The next morning Samantha went out to the oval for the workouts. Mike had told Len to tack up Sierra, and Samantha was looking forward to riding him to see what Mike had been talking about. She firmly believed that every horse would eventually respond if you approached it the right way.

But as soon as Len started leading the dark chestnut out of the barn, she could see she wasn't going to have a dull morning.

He skittered around at the end of the lead shank, and Len had to use a lot of muscle and persuasive words to keep the colt on all fours. Sierra was a good-looking animal, fairly tall with powerful hindquarters. His coat was the color of well-aged copper, almost mahogany, and he had no markings except for one white stocking on his right hind leg. He looked a lot like his sire, Maxwell, and Mike hoped he had the racing genes of his dam, the Secretariat mare. Sierra certainly seemed to have a strong-willed disposition, Samantha thought as Len led the colt over to the rail where she, her father, and Mike waited.

She reached out to stroke the colt's neck.

"Watch out," Len said mildly. "He's in a biting mood this morning. Nearly took a chunk out of me when I brought him out of his stall."

Samantha laid her hand gently on the colt's muzzle instead and looked him in the eye. "So, you're a handful, huh?" she said to the horse with a smile.

As he looked at her, Samantha could almost see the mischief in his brown eyes. He suddenly tossed up his head and pulled his lips back from his teeth, but Samantha was too quick for him. She grabbed the base of his reins beneath his chin, and between her hold and Len's hold on the lead, there was no way he could snatch out to bite her. "Gotcha," Samantha said.

Sierra huffed in indignation.

"We'll be friends yet," Samantha said firmly. "I don't think you're a meany. You're just too playful for your own good."

"No, he's not mean," Len confirmed. "More playful, but he sure likes his own way."

"You sure you want to try him out?" her father said. Samantha knew he still got a little nervous when she was in the saddle. He couldn't help but remember her mother's fatal accident.

"I'm sure," Samantha said. "Don't worry. You know I've ridden green and high-strung horses before."

"He's not entirely green," Mike said. "He's not stupid, and he knows what's expected of him out there. I'll warn you, though . . . he'll probably try to pitch you. But once he finds out he can't get rid of you that easily, he should settle down. Anyway, let's see if the feminine touch will make a difference," Mike added in a teasing tone.

"Okay, boy," she said, going to Sierra's left

side. "Let's see what you can do."

Len had pulled down the stirrups, and Mike gave Samantha a leg into the saddle. Sierra pranced beneath her and arched his neck as she settled in the saddle and gathered the reins in a tight hold. Len was still holding the lead shank. "Tell me when you're ready," he said.

A moment later, Samantha nodded. Len quickly unsnapped the lead, and Samantha gently urged Sierra through the gap. The colt's ears were pricked forward. He walked, with seeming innocence, onto the track, but Samantha prepared herself for fireworks. She pushed her heels down in her stirrup irons, wrapped her fingers in his mane, and gripped the colt's sides firmly with her legs. Sierra took a couple of brisk sidesteps across the harrowed dirt, and then immediately followed that maneuver with several bucking jumps up the track. But Samantha stuck like glue.

The colt seemed mystified that he still had a rider on his back, and irritated, too. He tried to break forward into a gallop, but Samantha had his reins firmly entwined in her fingers. He couldn't get the bit. Samantha sat back in the saddle, away from his withers, and made him settle into a collected canter. She would have preferred to warm him up at a trot, but she knew that pulling him back further might inspire more bucking.

Her hands, steady and firm on the reins, let him know that she was totally in control as they moved around the first sweeping turn of the oval. She decided to keep him in near the center of the track until he'd worked off some of his willfulness. Then she'd move him in closer to the rail.

They lapped the track. The exercise was working off some of Sierra's high spirits, but Samantha wasn't about to relax her guard. She gradually reined Sierra in closer to the inside rail. She could feel him fighting for rein and could feel the unleashed power of the animal beneath her. Yet Mike had said the colt was a disappointment.

"I know you have ability," Samantha murmured. "Why aren't you showing it?"

The colt's ears flicked back momentarily. Samantha had already noticed that the colt's ears had remained pricked forward—a sign that he wasn't paying attention to his rider. She smiled grimly to herself. There had to be a way to get him interested. He was fighting her constantly for more rein, but Samantha was beginning to understand that he was fighting for rein out of willfulness.

"Okay, let's see what you can do with more rein," she said, crouching in the saddle and giving him an inch. For an instant the colt was caught by surprise at having his own way; then he quickly changed gaits and burst forth at a gallop. "All right," Samantha said under her breath. "Now let's just settle down and go."

They moved fairly quickly through the next furlong, and he was still tugging at the rein. She let a little more out and felt him thrust his head forward, taking the extra rein. She settled down in the saddle, expecting him to continue going forward at the same pace, now that he had the rein he wanted. Because of all the surprises she'd pulled on him, his ears were pricked back now.

Samantha thought with satisfaction that maybe there *was* a way to get through to the colt. Then suddenly his ears pricked forward, he fell off the bit, and he started dawdling.

"Come on," she said, twitching the reins to get his attention. "What are you doing? Let's go!"

He continued galloping, but he was playing and refused to pick up the pace again. They practically sauntered through the remaining quarter of a mile, before Samantha gave up, rose in her stirrups, and pulled him back to a canter. Sierra was still full of energy, though, dancing sideways across the track. Samantha firmly pulled him back into a trot and headed him to the gap. She was boiling with frustration. What made the colt tick?

Mike shrugged his shoulders as Samantha rode Sierra off the track. "See what I mean?" he said.

Samantha huffed out a sigh and frowned thoughtfully. "He was a powerhouse early on, then, boom . . . nothing! You know what—I think he's bored. As long as he's testing you, he's interested, but as soon as you let him have his head, he loses interest."

Charlie had come to the oval during the workout. "There are horses who just don't want to lift a hoof on the track, no matter what you do, no matter what their breeding is."

"We've all come across them," Mr. McLean said in agreement.

"I just hate giving up on him," Mike said. "I mean I could always hold on to him for stud, or sell him if worse came to worst—he's got the bloodlines. But I think I'll give him a little more time."

Samantha agreed with Mike. She'd been attracted to the colt from the beginning, but she also knew the hard facts of trying to run a racing stable. Mike couldn't afford to keep a horse that wasn't producing. "I'll keep working with him if you want, Mike," she offered.

"You can work him anytime, Sammy, but are you going to have the time? The Preakness is less than two weeks away."

"You're right. I won't have a lot of extra time for a while," Samantha said. "I don't think you should give up on him, though."

"I won't—not yet."

7

IT HAD RAINED CONTINUALLY FOR TWO DAYS BEFORE the Preakness. On Friday Samantha and her father had arrived at the Pimlico track in Baltimore to a downpour. The skies had cleared on the morning of the race, but the track had still been heavy and wet when the field had gone to the post.

Samantha had been worried about the condition of the track, but Charlie had planned ahead. That morning he had had Pride reshod with mud caulks, shoes which would give him greater traction on a soft or sloppy track.

"Even if the track dries out," Charlie told Samantha, "the caulks won't hurt him, and I can't see this surface drying out by this afternoon."

The caulks had probably given Pride an extra

edge. For the second time he'd bested Ultrasound, who'd come in third. Carousel Delight, who was known to like an off track, had challenged Pride in the stretch, but Pride had fought back and beaten him! By one length, he had won the second leg of the Triple Crown, but the race had taken its toll on him.

"He's wiped out," Samantha said to Ashleigh as they stood outside Pride's stall the next morning. "He barely touched his feed last night or this morning."

"I know," Ashleigh said with a frown. "I was afraid he would be exhausted, but any horse would be tired after the race he put in. At least he'll have three weeks before the Belmont."

Samantha nodded. Pride would sure need the extra time to get back on his feet. "Have reporters been asking you and Charlie how he's come out of the race?" she asked.

"The reporters have been asking tons of questions," Ashleigh answered. "I'm following Charlie's example and keeping my mouth shut. I did talk to Mr. Townsend last night before he left, but he didn't seem worried about Pride's condition. He just said that he was confident Pride would bounce back after a few days' rest. When I told him that I've never seen Pride so worn out, he just said that the Belmont was too important a race to skip, and that Pride had to run—especially because winning the Belmont means winning the Triple Crown."

Samantha idly fingered a strand of her red hair. "I figured he'd say that. Even if Pride needs more of a rest, Mr. Townsend isn't going to miss the last leg of the Triple Crown. Pride's already guaranteed the million-dollar bonus, though, for winning two legs."

"I don't think it's just the money," Ashleigh said, "it's the prestige, too, though I'm pretty sure the Townsends are also thinking about the money. I heard Brad talking to another owner about investing in a very well bred two-year-old."

"And bragging his head off as usual," Samantha said, curling her lip. "Anyway, Pride can rest after the Belmont."

Ashleigh nodded. "No question about that. I wouldn't think of racing him again until the Travers in late August, and we'll baby him until the Belmont."

"Charlie's already given me some suggestions," Samantha said, "—a couple of easy walks a day, a daily massage, heat compresses or ice if he shows any soreness." Samantha straightened her shoulders in determination. "Don't worry, I'll give Pride the absolute best."

"You always do, Sammy," Ashleigh said. "I'm not worried about that." She paused. "Mr. Townsend wanted to ship him straight to New York and let him spend the time before the Belmont at the track. I talked him out of it, though. With Pride so tired, it would be crazy to bring him to a strange track. We can afford to fly him up from

Kentucky the week of the race. I'll pay for your airfare to fly up, too."

"No," Samantha protested. "I can pay with the bonus you gave me."

Ashleigh laughed. "Sammy, you don't seem to understand that you're worth your weight in gold when it comes to getting Pride relaxed and in the right mind-set before a race. And, believe me, I can afford it, after all he's been winning."

They vanned Pride back to Kentucky that afternoon. Samantha rode with him in the back, keeping the tired horse company. Charlie had had the track vet check Pride over before they left, and physically there was nothing wrong with the colt. He was just tired from the tremendous effort he'd put out during the race.

When they arrived back at Whitebrook that evening, Samantha led Pride to his stall, where Len was filling the hay net and water bucket. "That was some kind of a race, big fella," he said to Pride. "If you're tuckered out, I'm not surprised. But we'll see you get the best of everything. I hear from Charlie that he's off his feed," Len added to Samantha.

She nodded. "I thought I'd try to give him something now."

As she spoke, three sleepy cats came down the aisle from the direction of the tack room.

"Guess they heard you," Len said. "That kitten

sure has missed this guy. He keeps checking out the stall, then wanders away all sad when he finds it empty." Len gave her a wide smile. "It's nice to see how close these animals are."

At that moment, Samantha heard a chorus of purrs at her feet. Jeeves was curling around Len's legs; Snowshoe rubbed her head against Samantha's jeans; but Sidney was the loudest. He was looking at Pride, purring ecstatically. Suddenly, Sidney jumped from the bedding onto Pride's back, and the big colt craned his head around to watch as the kitten walked in a circle over his back, then settled down in a tight ball. Pride let out a slow, contented sigh.

"He's glad to be home," Len said. "I was afraid the Townsends would send him straight up north to Belmont. It's better that he's here."

"Yup, it is," Charlie said, striding up the aisle. He looked a little tired and drawn in the dim overhead lights.

"Charlie, are you all right?" Samantha asked with concern. She knew how many hours he'd worked over the weekend.

"I'm fine," Charlie said gruffly. "Nothing to worry about. I just wanted to check him out again before I head to bed. How's he doing? Eaten anything?"

Samantha glanced over her shoulder to see Pride tear a mouthful of hay from his net. She grinned. "It looks like he's started! I can tell he's relaxed since he got back here."

Charlie was looking at the kitten curled up on Pride's back. He shook his head, but Samantha noticed he was rubbing his hand over his mouth to hide his smile. He watched Pride grab another mouthful of hay, then nodded to himself. "I think the colt will be all right. You remember what I told you about the massages?" he said to Samantha.

"Uh-huh, I was going to give him one tonight."

Charlie nodded. "Then I'll be off. Len can help you if you need it. Night."

"Good night, Charlie."

"See you in a bit," Len said. "I don't know if you're hungry, but you can heat up that stew I left on the stove."

"Yup." Charlie shuffled off, and for the next half hour Samantha massaged Pride's muscles. She could almost feel the colt relaxing under her touch.

"I know, guy," she said softly, "you can't tell us where it hurts, but I'll try to guess, and in a few days you'll be feeling like yourself again."

Pride blew out a long breath, and as a sure sign of his comfort, his normally sharply pricked ears flopped sideways on his head a little. Sidney never moved from the curve of Pride's back. He just continued purring, which had a soothing effect on all of them.

"That should do it," Len said when Samantha's hands and arms were beginning to feel tired and sore. "He'll get a good sleep tonight. You can walk him in the morning, and if he shows any stiffness, we'll try compresses or ice and a little more massage. You've gotta be pretty tired yourself, Sammy."

Samantha nodded. The last three days had taken a toll on her, though she only let herself feel it now. She stifled a yawn with the back of her hand. "I guess I am tired, but it's been so exciting!"

"I know. There's nothing like winning two jewels in the Triple Crown." Len chuckled. "I was close once. I was grooming a horse who almost did it. Charlie's got to be feeling pretty good. This is some way to cap off his career. Neither of us is getting any younger."

"Is he all right, Len?" Samantha asked. "I was kind of worried about him tonight."

"You kidding? This kind of excitement is what makes Charlie come alive. He might be tired from it all, but, heck, at least he's a part of it. At our age, that's all you can ask for." He smiled. "You go in and get to bed now. I'll be here a little longer checking the horses. I'll make sure Pride's okay before I head in."

"Thanks, Len," Samantha said. She reached over the stall door to take Pride's head in her hands and kiss his nose. "Sleep tight, big guy. I love you."

Pride blew a sweet, hay-scented breath against her cheek, and Samantha left the barn with a final wave to Len.

When she got to the cottage, she found that her

91

father had dozed off on the couch with the television on, so Samantha quietly slipped into the kitchen to call Yvonne.

"Hi," Samantha said as quietly as she could.

"You're back!" Yvonne screeched into the telephone. Samantha pulled the receiver an inch away from her ear. "I've been waiting for you to call all night!" Yvonne cried.

"Shhh. I can hear you," Samantha said. "And my father's sleeping in the other room."

"Okay," Yvonne said, dropping her voice to an exaggerated stage whisper. "He won it! How are you feeling? I wish I'd been there! Oh, my God, all the television coverage! They say he's the next Secretariat. Did they talk to you? I saw you a little bit in the clip where you were leading Pride and Ashleigh off the track, before the Townsends butted in. Oh, Sam, this is really incredible!"

"No kidding." Samantha laughed, but then sobered quickly. "But he was really beat coming out of it. Ashleigh and I are kind of worried about him, though he's gotten better since he got home. He started eating . . . and you know that kitten, Sidney . . ."

They talked for another fifteen minutes, then Samantha hung up and headed to the refrigerator for a snack. But just as she opened the refrigerator door, the phone rang again. She rushed to answer it before the ringing woke up her father.

"Hello?" she said breathlessly.

"Did I get you at a bad time? It's Tor."

"No, it's okay," she said, thrilled to hear his voice. "We just got back tonight."

"Congratulations," Tor said. "Was the race as hard on him as it looked on TV? What an awful track!"

"It was hard. And he's pooped, but he'll be okay. I just worry about what the Belmont will take out of him."

"I thought you'd be more excited," Tor said. "The horse you trained has won two parts of the Triple Crown! You should be jumping around!"

"I would be, if I wasn't so tired," Samantha said with a smile.

"And you're worried about your horse, huh?"

"Yes. Wouldn't you be if it were Top Hat?'

"You bet I would." There was a moment of silence, then Tor went on in a rush. "I was going to ask you . . . but then I just realized you wouldn't be able to go anyway."

"Ask me what?"

"Well . . . I was going to ask you to go to the prom with me, but I think it's on the same weekend as the Belmont."

A blur of thoughts flashed through Samantha's mind. Tor had asked her to the prom! It was the last thing she'd expected. She was dumbstruck, but flattered, too—and excited! But the Belmont was so important—she had to be there for Pride. She couldn't miss the last leg of the Triple Crown for any reason, even to go to the prom with Tor.

"Tor, I'd like to go with you," she said, stumbling over her words, "but the Belmont—"

"Hey, you don't have to explain," he said quickly. "I'm lousy about keeping track of dates, and I didn't even think about the Belmont being the same weekend until I looked at the calendar just now. There's one hanging here by the phone."

"Tor, it's not that I don't want to go," Samantha said. "It's just that Pride is so important to me—I don't mean that you're—"

"Stop, Sammy," Tor said with a chuckle. "I understand."

"Do you?"

"Hey, of course. We'll do something another time. Listen, I know you're tired. I'll let you go and see you in school tomorrow."

"Okay. Good night, Tor. And thanks for asking me!" Samantha hung up, feeling dazed. Tor had asked her to the prom. He'd asked her on a date. Wow!

As she climbed the stairs to get ready for bed, she wondered what his invitation had meant. Had he asked her as a friend? Or did he like her more than that? Samantha had always thought of Tor as just a good friend, even though she'd recently had some strange feelings when she was around him. Now she was definitely beginning to think of him differently.

"GUESS WHO CALLED ME LAST NIGHT AFTER I TALKED TO you!" Yvonne said excitedly when she met Samantha at her locker the next morning. "Jay Schneider! He asked me to the junior prom!"

Samantha grinned. "All right! That's exactly what you wanted. And guess who called to ask me to the prom."

For an instant Yvonne just stared at Samantha, then she gasped. "Tor?"

"Yes! But I can't go. The prom's the same weekend as the Belmont."

"Oh gosh, that's right," Yvonne cried. "What a bummer! The prom *would* have to be the same weekend as the Belmont."

"I'm sure they didn't plan it that way," Samantha

95

said with a smile. "Tor understands how important the Belmont is to me, but it would have been fun to go." For some reason, Samantha was kind of nervous about seeing Tor that day in school. His invitation to the prom had somehow changed something in their relationship. How would he act? she wondered. How should she act?

"He'll ask you out again," Yvonne said confidently.

"Well, he *did* say we'd do something another time."

Yvonne giggled. "See, I told you he liked you. I knew he'd ask you out!"

"He probably only asked me because we're friends," Samantha said.

"Sure! You don't believe that any more than I do."

Just before lunch Tor caught up with Samantha in the hall. "Hi!" he said with one of his bright smiles.

A warm flush rose up Samantha's neck and suddenly she felt awkward, but Tor didn't seem to notice.

"I'm glad I found you before you sat down," he said quickly. "I've been thinking . . . how would you like to come to a show that Top Hat and I are competing in? It's in Louisville the week after the Belmont, and it's a pretty important one for us if we're going to qualify for the top ranks. I'll drive you over."

Samantha didn't have to think. She definitely

wanted to go. "I'd love to! I've never been to a big show, and I'd love to see you and Top Hat compete!"

Tor's smile seemed tinged with relief, or was that her imagination? Samantha wondered.

"I was hoping you could come," Tor said. "You'll enjoy it, I think, and you'll see some jumping that's a little more complicated than what you've seen at the stable."

"A *little* more complicated?" Samantha asked with a grin.

He grinned back, eyes dancing. "Well, quite a bit more complicated. I just hope Top Hat and I don't screw up—especially with you watching. Revise that—Top Hat never screws up . . . only his rider does."

"You won't mess up," Samantha said. From what she'd seen of Tor's riding in the stable, she knew he was a cool, concentrated, and outstanding rider. They continued talking about the show as they went into the cafeteria and joined the line of students waiting to get their lunches. "Do you get a case of nerves before a big show?" Samantha asked, thinking of how nervous she got before Pride's races.

He laughed. "You bet I do! I pace a lot, and I hear I get a little cranky. But usually I snap out of it when I get in the ring."

"I know what you mean," Samantha said. As she spoke, she saw Yvonne wave from a table across the cafeteria. She was sitting with Jay

97

Schneider, the boy who had asked her to the junior prom. Yvonne had met him in drama club and said he was an incredible actor.

"I think Yvonne might want to be left alone today," Samantha said.

Tor had noticed Yvonne and Jay, too. "I think you're right." He lifted his brows and smiled. "I hope he likes horses."

Samantha laughed. "He'd better if he's going to spend much time with Yvonne."

"So let's get a table by ourselves," Tor said.

Samantha nodded, feeling a touch of shyness, but she thought that was a very good idea.

Pride went back into light training the following week. Samantha was just preparing to take him out onto the oval one warm late-May morning when a Jeep Cherokee came down the drive. She recognized the Jeep as Clay Townsend's and wasn't surprised, since Mr. Townsend frequently came over to watch Pride's workouts.

She fastened the chin strap of her helmet and urged Pride out onto the oval. Then she spotted a second vehicle coming down the drive, a low-slung sports car—Brad's Ferarri. Samantha stiffened, startling Pride.

"Sorry, boy," she said quickly. She forced herself to relax again, but she wondered what Brad was doing there. He'd never come to Whitebrook before.

Samantha saw that Ashleigh had walked over to Mr. Townsend and knew that the older girl couldn't be too happy with Brad's appearance either. Samantha tried to put her mind to business. Pride's workouts leading up to the Belmont were too important to let Brad's arrival upset her concentration.

"Okay, Pride," she said, "let's warm up." Pride, obedient as usual, stepped right out into an energetic trot at her urging. Samantha did her best to put everything else from her mind as she trotted the colt around the first turn of the mile track. After a half-mile, she gave him the signal to canter, and they moved at that gait through the next half-mile. She was repeating the training plan that had worked so well before the Preakness, giving Pride several works at a slow gallop, then a couple of sharpening-up breezes before Pride was shipped to the track.

Out of the corner of her eye, she saw Charlie, Ashleigh, and the Townsends gathered along the outside rail. Her father and Mike were behind them with a couple of horses that would be worked next. She readied herself, then dropped lower in the saddle over Pride's withers and gave him rein. "Let's gallop!" she called.

Pride had gradually snapped back over his week of complete rest, but Samantha knew the big colt needed time to regain his strength to be at his best for the grueling mile-and-a-half test of the Belmont Stakes.

Pride broke into a gallop. They lapped the track,

with Pride's hoofbeats sounding a steady rhythm on the dirt. Even at a slow gallop, Pride's long strides ate up ground. Samantha lapped the track once more, alert for any signs of weariness in the colt—any signs that he was pushing himself. Stamina would be important in the longer distance of the Belmont. Front-end speed wouldn't be, and she, Ashleigh, and Charlie had already talked of trying to pace Pride in the big race, letting others go ahead to set the early pace. Whether Pride would let another horse in front was the big question.

Samantha was satisfied with the workout as she stood in the stirrups and pulled Pride back into a canter, then a trot. Then she turned him and trotted back to the gap where the others were standing. Pride came out of the work in good shape. Although he hadn't shown his usual fire, he didn't seem overly stressed, and his bright coat wasn't marred by sweat.

Charlie looked satisfied as Samantha rode toward the group, but Ashleigh and Brad were exchanging some sharp comments.

"Do you mean you're just starting to gallop him *now*?" Brad said to Ashleigh. "With only a week and half to go till the Belmont?"

"He needed the rest," Ashleigh shot back. "He was beat after the Preakness. If we'd pushed his workouts, he'd never have been in shape for the race."

"I don't see that he's going to be in shape this

way either," Brad said coldly. There was an arrogant scowl on his handsome face that marred his good looks.

"This is exactly how we worked him up to the Preakness," Ashleigh told him. "And, with the off track, that was a very tough race on him. If anything, he needs more of a rest than we've given him."

"You don't seem to realize," Brad sneered, "that he's running for the third leg of the Triple Crown—"

Ashleigh cut him short. "I realize that perfectly, and that's why we're training him this way."

Clay Townsend stepped over to them. "Charlie and Ashleigh have done a good job with his training so far," he said. "I don't see any need to change the game plan."

Brad's scowl deepened. "When are you flying him up?" he asked Charlie.

"Monday," Charlie said, giving Brad a level, unflinching stare.

"I still say he should be up there now." Brad turned and headed back to his Ferarri. A moment later the powerful engine roared, and gravel spit as Brad gunned it up the drive.

"The colt will bounce back," Mr. Townsend said to Charlie, ignoring his son's behavior. "He always does. I don't need to tell you how important winning this next one is."

As Samantha dismounted, she noticed the scowl on Ashleigh's face. The older girl was probably thinking the same thing as Samantha. For the Townsends, winning the Triple Crown had become the only objective, and Pride's well-being was becoming less and less important. To be fair, though, Samantha knew that Clay Townsend was not a negligent horseman. He'd never in the past jeopardized a horse's health just to win. That was some consolation, and of course, Ashleigh would be in Pride's saddle on race day, riding the race with Pride in mind. But the pressure would be on her to win. Even newspapers that didn't normally devote much attention to horse racing were trumpeting Pride. The hopes and dreams of a lot of people were resting on the colt.

Ashleigh walked over as Samantha was preparing to lead Pride back to the stable. "Why does Brad have to come over here and stick his two cents in?" Ashleigh muttered. "I don't know how he can show his face after all the trouble he's caused in the past."

"He's got too big an ego to blame himself for any mess he's created," Samantha said. "He's probably twisted everything around."

Ashleigh shook her head and laid a gentle hand on Pride's shoulder. "How'd he feel?" she asked. "I didn't want to ask in front of the Townsends. It looked to me like he was more subdued than usual."

"He hasn't come back all the way yet," Samantha agreed. "He did what I asked willingly, but he didn't have that extra spark."

"That's what I thought, but I'm sure we're

doing the right thing working him lightly now, and he's been eating better."

"Like a champ. He's put back on most of the weight he lost after the Preakness, and he looks healthy—look at the shine on his coat," Samantha said proudly.

"Winning five big races in less that six months would take a lot out of any horse," Ashleigh said. "Just hang in there for one more race, Pride," she added gently, "and you can have a nice long rest, with nothing to do but eat and relax."

Pride nickered, and Samantha dropped a kiss on his nose, then went to his side to untack him.

By Monday, when Pride was scheduled to fly up to Belmont, he had snapped back amazingly. His step was springy when he went out on the track, and though they hadn't asked him to do more than light gallops, he was showing his old energy and desire to run. Samantha had spent hours with the colt in preparation for the race, lavishing him with attention, massaging him, grooming him, and pampering him with a special feed mix that Charlie had concocted. It all seemed to work, but none of them kidded themselves into thinking the race ahead would be an easy romp for Pride.

"So Pride left this morning," Tor said when he, Samantha, and Yvonne met at school.

Samantha nodded. "Ashleigh and Charlie are

flying up with him. They'll give him a day to adjust to his new surroundings, then Ashleigh plans to breeze him on Wednesday and Thursday. It'll give him a chance to get used to the Belmont surface and the track layout."

"You wish you were there, though, don't you?" Tor said sympathetically.

"Don't I ever!" Samantha looked over at him and saw from his expression that he understood exactly how she felt. She was also feeling strangely elated because he'd told her the day before that he wasn't going to the prom after all. He and his father were going to a local horse show instead. "Ashleigh told me she'd call every night, but I want to be with Pride and see what's going on firsthand."

"You're afraid Brad Townsend's going to butt in again?" Yvonne asked.

"He'll be there," Samantha said. "He and his father flew up over the weekend."

"Well, there'll be plenty of people cheering for you here. And I bet I'll see you on TV again. My friend, the star!" Yvonne teased.

Samantha laughed. "Get out of here. And even if Pride wins, you'll be lucky if you see me. Brad and Lavinia will have to be in the photos," she said in the same marble-mouthed tone she'd heard Lavinia use. Both girls started giggling.

"But we'll know who deserves most of the credit," Tor told her. "You."

9

THE NEW YORK SKYLINE WAS HIGHLIGHTED BY A RED-skied sunset as the plane circled before landing. Samantha stared out the window, taking in every bit of the scene below—the Manhattan skyscrapers, the many bridges, and the water surrounding the islands.

Ashleigh was waiting as Samantha stepped through the gate into the airport terminal. On a Friday night, the terminal was packed with people bustling in all directions. Samantha liked the novelty of so many scurrying bodies. Although she'd certainly seen crowds at the track, life on the outskirts of Lexington, Kentucky, was quiet in comparison.

"I just brought this one bag," Samantha said to

Ashleigh, hoisting the handles of her large duffle over her shoulder, "so I don't have to collect any luggage."

"Good thinking," Ashleigh said. "I've rented a car for the week, and I even managed to find a parking place that isn't miles away from the terminal. Before you ask, Pride's fine," she added, but then Ashleigh's brow furrowed for a second.

"What's wrong?"

"Nothing really," Ashleigh answered. "I'm just a little worried about how much this race will take out of him."

"You said he had two good breezes."

"He did, but remember, this is a mile-and-a-half race. There'll be some fresh horses running, too. One's being shipped in from England, another from France. A fresh horse will have an advantage over Pride, who's run in two big races in the last month."

Samantha nodded. She had already scrutinized the charts of all the entrants in the Belmont, and she knew both of the foreign horses had decent records in their own countries. "But they'll have disadvantages, too," she told Ashleigh. "The long trip . . . and neither one of them is used to running on the dirt or on an oval."

"We'll just have to keep our fingers crossed," Ashleigh said. "You've been to Belmont before, haven't you?"

"Only once. My father usually worked in Florida

and Kentucky, but we all came up here when one of his owners decided to race his string here for a season. I was pretty young, though. I don't think I got more than a mile from the track and the motel room we stayed in. I was only interested in the horses anyway."

Ashleigh smiled. "That sounds like you. Oh, by the way, I hope you don't get upset, but I've set up an interview for you tomorrow."

"What?" Samantha exclaimed. "Me? Who with?"

"A woman reporter for a big Long Island paper. Human interest, she said. Even though you haven't gotten a lot of credit yet, Sammy, people know how big a part you've played in Pride's training. Oh, and thanks for sending me a copy of the high school newspaper. That was a super article you wrote about the Derby!"

Samantha flushed a little. "Thanks. I really like writing the articles, and the kids at school seem to enjoy them. Ash, you wouldn't believe how many people came up to me today to wish Pride luck. Even some of my teachers. It's really amazing!"

"I remember that feeling from when Wonder was racing," Ashleigh said. "This is going to be a big weekend. It's getting absolutely nuts at the track, with the Belmont and the Nassau County Handicap both on Saturday. And the possibility of a new Triple Crown winner has everybody hyper. I hope it doesn't affect Pride."

They stopped at the track backside before going to the motel room, which Samanatha would be sharing with Ashleigh. The Belmont facilities were impressive, with well-kept grounds and acres of stabling. Samantha and Ashleigh had to hike quite a distance before they got to the barn where Pride and several allowance horses the Townsends had shipped up were stabled. The barn area was fairly quiet, though grooms, trainers, and several owners still roamed about in the warm evening air.

Charlie was sitting on a folding chair outside Pride's stall, talking to his old friend, Hank, the head groom at Townsend Acres. Hank gave Samantha a wide smile.

"Long time no see," he said. "But you've sure been busy."

"Hi, Hank," Samantha said cheerfully. "Hi, Charlie."

Charlie nodded. "Good flight?"

"Fine. What do you think of Pride, Hank?" she asked. "He's filled out a little since you saw him last."

"He's looking good," Hank answered. "He's turned out every bit as good as I expected when he was a yearling and two-year-old."

"I have to go in and say hello to him," Samantha said, unlatching the top half of the stall door, which Charlie had closed to give the colt some quiet. Pride was dozing in the back of the thickly bedded box stall, but as soon as the light filtered into the stall, he started to alertness.

"It's me, boy," Samantha called softly. "I finally got here. I've missed you!"

Sleepy though he was, Pride pricked his ears and gave a delighted whicker. Samantha let herself into the stall, and the colt stepped toward her, nuzzling his velvet nose into her shoulder and making soft noises of greeting. Samantha took his head in her hands and rubbed her cheek against his. "I'm glad to see you, too," she said, feeling choked up at Pride's welcome. "I won't keep you awake now, though. We have a big day tomorrow, and you'll need all the rest you can get." She looked the colt over in the dim light, and she was happy with what she saw. His coat was silken, with a deep and healthy sheen. The ribs that had started to show after the Preakness were smoothly filled in, and his muscles had the solid tone of an athlete in top shape.

"You're looking great," she said, giving him a last hug. "I'll be here first thing in the morning, but you go back to sleep now." Pride nickered and blew softly into her hand. Reluctantly Samantha left the stall and carefully latched it behind her.

"I know Charlie and Ashleigh are kind of concerned about the race tomorrow," Hank said, "but if he performs as well as he looks, I don't think you've got anything to worry about."

"We'll see," said Charlie with his usual pessimism. "Well," he added, pushing himself up from the chair, "I'm heading for the sack, and you two girls ought to do the same. It'll be an early morning."

"We're heading right back to the motel," Ashleigh said. "Though I'm wondering how well I'm going to be able to sleep."

Samantha was wondering the same thing. Already she could feel nervous and excited butterflies in her stomach.

By the middle of the next afternoon, Samantha's head was spinning. She'd done her interview late in the morning, and she thought it had gone okay. The woman interviewing her had been nice and had wanted to know all the details of how Samantha had begun helping with Pride's training. When Samantha described the special bond she felt with Pride, the reporter seemed to know exactly what she meant. "This is going to make a wonderful human-interest story," she'd told Samantha in parting.

The Townsends had been by the stall early in the afternoon, showing off Pride to friends of theirs. All of them were expensively dressed, including Lavinia, who hung on Brad's arm constantly. The dozens of other curious spectators were kept at a distance by Charlie and Hank.

Reporters and television crew carrying video cameras buzzed around the backside, talking to anyone who had a connection to Pride.

Samantha tried to ignore the cameras and the crowds, but when she and Charlie took Pride out for a walk, she could tell the colt was beginning to react to all the excitement. His nostrils flared as he sniffed the air and took in the hectic scene, and he turned his head from side to side as they walked. And the day was growing hot and humid. The heat wasn't unbearable, but the stickiness in the air seemed to make everyone feel lethargic. Pride, too, seemed listless, even when Samantha bathed him after their walk and put him back in his shaded and well-ventilated stall. But Samantha knew horses were cold-weather animals and were sensitive to excessive heat.

She noticed Charlie scowling as he studied Pride, but knew that was the old trainer's usual prerace expression. Just the same, Samantha asked him if he was concerned.

The old trainer took off his hat to wipe his brow with the red bandana he always carried. "If the heat's bothering him, it'll be bothering all the other horses, too," he said. "Can't be helped, though I would have liked the temperature ten degrees cooler."

Ashleigh came by after Samantha had settled Pride back in his stall. Samantha only had to take one look at Ashleigh's face to know the older girl was getting her own set of jitters.

"I'm so antsy I can't sit still," Ashleigh said. "Now that he's settled, why don't you take a walk with me around the barns. I want to take another look at those European horses."

Samantha quickly agreed. She couldn't sit still either, and there was nothing left for her to do. Pride's tack was spotless, and everything was ready for the race.

"He's not usually this mopey before a race," Ashleigh said worriedly as they wove their way between the stabling barns.

"Charlie thinks it's because of the heat."

"I went out to see how the track was playing," Ashleigh said, "and I talked to some of the jockeys after the first two races. It's fast, but there seems to be a bias against the inside lane. I'll have to keep him off the rail, though the track could change before race time. It's already going to be harder on him with the ten post position. I'll have to get him out fast and make up early ground to beat the traffic." She heaved a sigh. "Everyone's expecting so much of him! If he doesn't win, people are going to be mad. I wish Mike would get here. His flight must have been delayed."

"He'll be here," Samantha assured her.

"I know," Ashleigh said with an attempt at a smile.

People recognized Ashleigh as they moved through the barns. They called out and waved and asked about Pride. "He's fine—just fine," Ashleigh called back, disguising her own worries with a cheerful smile. "Here's the English horse, Super Value," she said to Samantha, pointing to a stall that was surrounded by curious fans and reporters. The stall door was open, and big bay colt had his head over the door, his ears pricked.

"He sure looks alert," Samantha said with disma. "He's only run on the dirt once, though."

Ashleigh nodded. "But he won, and European horses are used to running longer distances. The French horse is in the next row over."

The French horse, Champagne, had been bred in Kentucky. He was a darker bay with an irregular white blaze. "He's small," Samantha said. "Though I know that doesn't always mean anything."

Before they went back to Pride's stall, they took a look at the other entrants in the Belmont. Ultrasound, Knightshade, and Ricky's Charmer were all running. So was Carousel Delight, though few gave him much of a chance on a good track. The West Coast horse, Count Abdul, was racing after having skipped the Preakness, and the track would be to his liking. Samantha was afraid of another speed duel, and she knew Ashleigh would be, too. Other entrants in the field had skipped either the Derby or the Preakness and would all be fresher than Pride and the other horses who'd gone the whole Triple Crown route.

Mike was waiting at Pride's stall when they returned, and Ashleigh ran to meet him and give him a hug. Samantha said hello to him, but then she set out to give Pride a meticulous final grooming.

She talked to him as she worked. "I know you'll perk up when it's time to go out to the track. This has been a tough month, hasn't it? But I believe in you. You'll do you're absolute best. You always do." Pride turned his head to nuzzle her. "If only there wasn't all this awful pressure!"

When Samantha emerged from the stall, the Townsends were there with several other people, including Lavinia. Every hair on Lavinia's blond head was brushed neatly in place, and Samantha unconsciously brushed back the damp red strands that had come loose from her ponytail. While Mr. Townsend talked to Ashleigh and Charlie, Samantha heard Brad bragging to his guests. "No question he's the best colt we've had since Townsend Prince," he said.

Samantha felt her lip curling and turned her back on Brad and the visitors. She stowed her brushes in Pride's tack box and waited for Charlie to give her the signal to bring the colt out. A moment later, he did.

Samantha took the lead shank from outside the stall and clipped it to Pride's halter. "All set, big guy?" she said softly. "I'll be waiting for you in the saddling paddock."

Pride nickered, and Samantha led him out. The satin sheet she had pulled over him emphasized his sleek, muscular build. Where it showed, his copper coat gleamed like a newly minted penny, and his long mane and tail fell like silken threads.

"You're right, Brad," Lavinia said. "He's in superb shape. He's sure to win."

What would *she* know? Samantha thought in disgust. What could that spoiled rich girl know of the loving hours Samantha, Ashleigh, and Charlie had put in to get Pride to this point?

Then Charlie was taking Pride's lead. "See you in a bit," he said to Samantha.

"We'll meet you at the paddock," Mr. Town-send told Ashleigh. "Come on," he added jovially to the others. "We'll need to get up to our seats if we're going to watch the Nassau County Handicap."

"Well, Sammy," Ashleigh said. "Here's hoping."

Samantha nodded and sighed heavily, wishing her stomach would stop jumping around.

After she had showered and changed into clean jeans and a T-shirt, Samantha proceeded to the saddling area and readied Pride's tack. Then she studied each of the horses in the field as they arrived. Some showed signs of overexcitement as they eyed the mob encircling the walking ring and paddock.

Pride drew the most attention as Charlie led him to their box. The crowd loudly cheered and whistled. Pride was more alert than he had been earlier in the day. He snorted and stared out at the commotion, shifting his feet beneath him.

"Easy, boy," Samantha soothed as Charlie tacked up the colt.

"Get him out there and walk him around a little," he told Samantha. "I see the Townsends are here." He jerked his thumb in the direction of the television cameras. Samantha glanced over and saw Mr. Townsend and Brad being interviewed by the commentator for one of the big networks.

Several other horses and their grooms were already in the walking ring. Samantha saw Super Value dancing eagerly at the end of his shank. The big bay was obviously on his toes. Ultrasound was in the ring, too, although he followed his groom more complacently. Samantha knew he would be as tired as Pride going into the race, but the fast track, which most likely would mean a fast pace, would help him. The track was also suited to Count Abdul, and Samantha saw that the roan colt looked fresh as he was led into the ring.

The Townsends had left the television crew and had gone to talk to Charlie. Samantha wondered if there was some kind of disagreement going on, because Charlie's lips were pursed and he was shaking his head at something Brad had said.

The jockeys had come into the ring to join the owners and trainers of the mounts they were riding. Ashleigh was one of them, looking trim and professional in her green and gold silks. She nodded to the Townsends, but her eyes were on Pride. The colt was growing more excited now, bobbing his head and prancing, and Samantha noticed with dismay that patches of sweat were already darkening his coat. With the heat and humidity, it wasn't surprising, but Pride didn't usually break out in a sweat before a race.

The call came for jockeys to mount, and Samantha walked Pride to where Ashleigh and Charlie stood. The Townsends were watching from just behind them. The old trainer ran his eyes over the colt, and Samantha could tell he didn't like the sweat patches. He spoke to Ashleigh after he gave her a leg into the saddle. "Try to give him the easiest trip you can," he said. "You're going to have to move him up fast out of the gate, but try to let someone else make the pace. The way the track's been playing, your best bet is to stay off the rail a bit—maybe sit back in second or third. I know it's not going to be easy holding him, but you've got a mile and a half to travel, the longest he's ever gone. Keep that in mind and try to reserve something for the end."

117

Ashleigh nodded, then spoke firmly. "But, Charlie, if I feel him tiring, I'm not going to push him. I'm not taking the chance of injuring him, even if it means losing the race."

Charlie made no comment, but Samantha could see from his face that he agreed. She led Pride and Ashleigh forward for another loop around the walking ring. "I don't like the way he's sweating up," Samantha said quietly to Ashleigh.

"It could be the heat, but I don't like it either," Ashleigh said, gently patting Pride's neck.

The field started moving out of the walking ring, and Samantha led Pride and Ashleigh out after the others. They were met by the outrider who would lead Pride onto the track. Samantha dropped a kiss on Pride's nose. "Just do your best, big guy. No one expects miracles of you."

The colt huffed out a sweet breath, and Samantha handed the lead shank up to the outrider. "Good luck," she said to Ashleigh.

Ashleigh managed a tight, nervous smile. "Thanks, Sammy."

Samantha, Charlie, and Mike didn't speak as they watched the field warm up from their grandstand seats. Pride looked good and was moving smoothly. He'd received a rousing cheer from the crowd as he'd passed the stands during the post parade. They loved him, but would they love him if he didn't win? Samantha wondered. Fans could be so fickle, especially when they held a losing ticket on a horse in whom they had placed all their hopes.

Samantha was so tense, she didn't even feel the trickles of perspiration sliding down the back of her neck.

"Ashleigh looks like she's sitting cool," Mike said nervously.

"She always puts her mind to business," Charlie told him.

Then the horses started loading into the gate. Ashleigh and Pride circled, waiting their turn. When it finally came, a gate assistant led Pride into the number-ten slot, and he went in calmly.

"Two horses to load," the announcer told the crowd, "Ricky's Charmer and Big Ben. Big Ben is in, all horses in place—and they're off! Count Abdul breaks cleanly from the three spot and heads right for the lead. Wonder's Pride is out quickly—but wait . . . Ricky's Charmer appears to have lugged in, bumping Wonder's Pride. But Wonder's Pride has recovered and is striding toward the lead. As they head into the Clubhouse Turn, it's Count Abdul, Knightshade, the French horse Champagne, Wonder's Pride just in back of them in fourth, then Super Value, Carousel Delight, Ricky's Charmer. Ultrasound as usual is running well off the pace. The field is moving out

119

of the Clubhouse Turn, but they still have a mile to go in this mile-and-a-half race. Count Abdul is setting fairly brisk fractions—twenty-three and two-fifths for the quarter-mile, a shade over forty-five for the half.

"Champagne, who has been under a strong hold by his jockey, is moving up on Knightshade to challenge Count Abdul, but the California horse is holding his lead by a half-length. Wonder's Pride, winner of the Derby and Preakness, is still back in fourth. Ashleigh Griffen is patiently holding him off the pace. It looks like she's trying new tactics for this race."

Samantha had her binoculars to her eyes, but because of the crush of horses tearing down the backstretch, she didn't have a clear view of Pride. She could see the green and gold of Ashleigh's silks, but she couldn't see enough of Pride to know if he was fighting Ashleigh for rein. There was also the awful possibility that Pride wasn't pushing to gain the lead at all, but Samantha wouldn't allow herself to think of that.

She, Mike, and Charlie all hunched forward in their seats, watching intently.

Champagne moved up to run neck and neck with Count Abdul. Knightshade dropped back slightly, and Samantha's breath caught in her throat when she saw Pride dropping back with him. He was still running just off Knightshade's

120

flank in fourth. "What's going on?" she said with a gasp.

Then Samantha finally got a clear view of Pride and let her breath out slowly. Pride was definitely fighting for rein, and Ashleigh was holding the big chestnut with all her strength.

But challengers were now moving up from all sides as the field headed to the far turn. In such a long race, it was important not to let your mount out too soon, Samantha knew. Ashleigh glanced back under her arm, but Samantha could see what Ashleigh couldn't. Ultrasound was in gear and moving up rapidly from the back of the pack. Super Value was weaving through horses. A long shot, Omnius, was coming up the gap most riders had left along the rail.

"The rail's getting faster," Samantha muttered under her breath. "That four horse is moving right up!"

"Wait and see," Charlie answered.

"And as they go into the far turn," the announcer cried with growing excitement, "Champagne has taken the lead from Count Abdul. Count Abdul is fighting back, but here comes Omnius up along the rail, putting a nose in front of Knightshade. Wonder's Pride is on Knightshade's flank, now back in fifth. Super Value has found an opening behind them! Ultrasound is roaring up on the outside!"

Samantha clutched her knees with white-knuckled hands and hunched farther forward. They were nearly into the stretch, and Ashleigh still hadn't made a move!

"God, she's sitting cool," Mike cried. "Oh, Ash, I hope you know what you're doing."

"She does," Charlie barked back. "Have some faith in her. She'll still have some horse under her when they're into the stretch."

Samantha prayed Charlie was right, because both Ultrasound and Super Value were right on Pride's heels. Then, just as Samantha was beginning to think that Pride didn't have anything left, the big chestnut started inching up out of fifth, into fourth, putting Knightshade away and gaining on Omnius.

"He's moving! He's moving!" Samantha cried, her voice hoarse.

"Wonder's Pride has started to make his move on the leaders," the announcer went on. "He's coming on strong up outside of Count Abdul and Champagne! As they turn into the stretch, the big chestnut is effortlessly putting them away! Count Abdul is finished. He's dropping back. Ultrasound continues his drive four-wide, and Super Value is moving up between horses."

"Go, Pride! Come on, boy!" Samantha screamed.

"They're at the eighth pole, and the Derby and Preakness winner now has a two-length lead!

Ultrasound still has six lengths to make up, and it doesn't look like he's going to catch Wonder's Pride. The others are dropping out of it, and Wonder's Pride now has a three-length lead—under a hand ride! We may be seeing our next Triple Crown champion today!" The announcer was growing hoarse in his excitement. "But wait—here comes the English colt! Super Value has just split horses, coming through a gap between Champagne and Count Abdul—and he's eating up ground! As they approach the sixteenth pole, he's up into second, only two lengths off Wonder's Pride! Has Ashleigh Griffen even seen this new challenger?"

"No!" Samantha screamed in horror as she saw the English horse continue to move up. She knew Ashleigh couldn't have seen their new challenger. But suddenly Ashleigh glanced back. Maybe she'd heard the approach of pounding hoofs, Samantha thought, but she was afraid it was too late!

Ashleigh kneaded her hands up along Pride's neck, and the colt reacted instantly. He fought back with a vengeance, pouring out more speed, and the two horses roared down the stretch.

"A breathtaking stretch drive!" the announcer screamed. "Wonder's Pride not giving an inch! Super Value, the fresh horse who hasn't raced in a month, continuing to challenge on the outside. Now he gets a nose in front. But Wonder's Pride comes back at him to get *his* nose in front. A fight to the finish here! A true show of courage from the Derby and Preakness champion! And Ashleigh Griffen hasn't touched him with her whip! They're at the wire! Too close to call! A photo finish! An unbelievable finish to this year's Triple Crown!"

Samantha had tears in her eyes. Pride had just demonstrated every ounce of heart he possessed. He had put in an incredible performance against a horse who had come into the race rested and in top form. Mike turned and gave her a hug. "Let's hope he had a few hairs of his nose in front," he said. "But whatever happens, he's showed he's a superstar."

"Let's get down there," Charlie said. He was so preoccupied, he hadn't bothered to replace his hat, which was still clenched in his hand.

By the time they reached the area near the winner's circle, the big board on the infield stopped flashing "Photo." Samantha's throat was so tight, she felt sick. Mike and Charlie froze beside her, waiting for the official order of finish to be flashed. And then the numbers of the first three finishers appeared. Three, Ten, Five. Super Value had won the photo!

A loud groan rippled through the crowd, and there were some angry shouts. Samantha felt a crushing disappointment. Pride had lost.

After that valiant fight, he'd lost by a head bob. The announcer was describing the finish. "The barest fraction of a nose, ladies and gentlemen, was all that stood in the way of a Triple Crown winner. A breathtaking race. A truly courageous effort!"

The sight of Pride and Ashleigh on the track brought Samantha out of her dazed state. She had a job to do. She started forward to meet them and lead Pride off the track as Super Value took his place in the winner's circle.

Samantha had barely reached Ashleigh's and Pride's side when Brad Townsend stormed up. "You let him lose it!" he called furiously to Ashleigh. "You deliberately lost it! He could have put out a little more. You never even *lifted* your whip! What were you carrying it for? *You're* responsible for this fiasco!"

10

AS SAMANTHA AND ASHLEIGH STARED AT BRAD WITH gaping mouths, Charlie strode up purposefully. "This isn't the place," he said to Brad in a tone that brooked no argument. "You want to talk about the race, we'll do it on the backside. Right now we have a colt to take care of, and if I'm not mistaken, you and your father are supposed to be at ceremonies to collect a million-dollar bonus check."

For a moment Brad glared at the old trainer, then he seemed to become aware of the crowds and reporters only yards away. He turned on his heel and left the track, but his angry comments hadn't gone unnoticed. Samantha saw dozens of people looking in their direction, including a few reporters.

"Let's get out of here before any more fireworks start," Charlie said. "Go weigh in," he told Ashleigh. "We'll meet you at the gap."

Mike joined them and gave Ashleigh a worried look. "Are you all right?"

Ashleigh dismounted and removed Pride's saddle, her eyes glittering with anger. "Fine," she answered tightly.

"He's crazy, Ash," Samantha said, trying to console the older girl.

"I just can't believe it," Ashleigh said grimly. "How dare he! And did he even think once of Pride? Pride put every ounce of heart into that race!"

"We know," Charlie said. "We'll sort it out."

Samantha had already thrown Pride's reins over his head and had started leading the exhausted colt forward. The sooner she got him off the track, the better. His coat was heavily specked with lathered sweat, and his head hung low, showing how spent he was from his effort. As Ashleigh hurried off with the saddle to weigh in, Charlie and Mike walked with Samantha and Pride to the backside.

"What's going on with that guy?" Mike asked angrily. "To make a scene like that on the track?"

"They lost the Triple Crown," Samantha said. "I think that's all Brad cared about."

"But look at the race this guy put in," Mike growled. "Look at how much it took out of him—

128

and he was running against a fresh horse!"

"You don't have to tell me," Samantha said.

"Well, I'd get ready for some fireworks at the barn," Charlie put in. "You can let me handle it, though maybe Townsend will have talked some sense into his kid by then."

Ashleigh met them as they headed to the barn area. Her face and her silks were liberally spattered with track dirt, but she was in no state of mind to head to the jockeys' rooms to change.

Mike immediately put his arm around her shoulders. "Ash, aren't you going to collect the bonus check?" he asked. "You're entitled to half of it."

"I'll get my half, but I'm too upset to go to any ceremony where I have to say nice things and smile for the camera. Especially if Brad's there."

"Ignore the jerk," Mike said, dropping a kiss on her cheek. Samantha saw tears welling up in Ashleigh's eyes.

"But what more could Brad ask?" Ashleigh cried. "No, I didn't use my whip, but Pride was already giving it everything he had all on his own!"

"We could see that," Samantha told her.

"Oh, I don't know," Ashleigh said, sighing. "Maybe if I'd seen that other horse coming up on us sooner—"

"Don't start blaming yourself," Charlie barked. "You gave him a perfect ride. You couldn't have done more." Even as Charlie spoke, he was keeping a watchful eye on Pride, studying the colt's movement for any sign of strain. Samantha had been studying the colt, too, and thought that aside from his obvious weariness, he seemed to have come out of the race sound. Later, a vet would check him over thoroughly, of course.

There were plenty of backside staff lining the route to the barn, and they called out encouraging words. Samantha was relieved that the reporters hadn't arrived yet, and they made it to the area outside Pride's stall without too much interruption.

Samantha immediately set to work on Pride, dribbling sponges of cool water over his back while Charlie checked the colt's legs and feet. Pride let out a long huffing grunt in pleasure. As Ashleigh, Mike, and Charlie talked about the race, Samantha sponged every inch of the colt, removing track dirt and sweat, until the copper sheen of his coat was visible again. She was beginning to remove the excess moisture from his coat with a sweat strap when Brad Townsend stormed up. Here we go, Samantha thought. She saw from Brad's expression that his mood hadn't improved.

"So you're here," Brad said to Ashleigh.

"Where else would I be?" she asked shortly. "I had to see how Pride came out of the race. Not that you care, but he's beat."

Brad didn't even look over at the colt. "What

was the meaning of that ride? And don't tell me the colt was already giving all he had. I heard you tell Charlie you wouldn't push him, even if it meant losing the race! You could have won that race! But instead you cost Townsend Acres the Triple Crown!"

"Townsend Acres?" Ashleigh shot back. "Have you forgotten that I own half of Pride, Brad? Just look at him! Does he look like a horse who had a lot in reserve? He's exhausted. He was tired before he even came into this race, and he went down nose and nose to the finish with a fresh horse! How much do you expect of him? Do you want him to race again? Or would you rather he dropped in his tracks?"

"He wouldn't have dropped in his tracks," Brad shouted. "A sting of the whip, and he would have had one extra jump on Super Value. You should hear what the press are saying!"

"I'd *love* to hear what the press are saying," Ashleigh answered. "I'm sure they're saying he put in one heck of an effort!"

"Don't be so sure. There are plenty of disappointed fans wondering why you *hand-rode* him through a near dead heat!"

Samantha glanced to Mike and was sure that at any second he was going to slam his fist into Brad's handsome face.

Fortunately Charlie stepped between them.

"That's enough. As far as I'm concerned, Ashleigh did just as she should. And I think your father will see it that way, too."

At that moment Mr. Townsend walked up. From the scowl on his face, it was obvious that he was very upset. He spoke directly to Ashleigh. "Brad tells me that you had no intention of pushing the colt, even if it meant losing the race! He heard you telling Charlie that in the walking ring."

"That's right," Ashleigh said defiantly.

"You took it upon yourself to make a decision like that?" he asked incredulously.

"Look at him!" Ashleigh motioned to Pride, and Mr. Townsend turned and walked over to the colt, nodding to Samantha as he did. Pride's head still hung low in weariness. Mr. Townsend tightened his mouth and turned back to Ashleigh.

"All right, he does look like the race has taken a lot out of him. But I still think that, with a crack or two of the whip, he could have won it."

"And maybe not raced again for a very long time," Ashleigh told him.

"I seriously doubt that would have happened," he said, annnoyed. "But since we haven't got the race to run over again, we'll never know. Frankly, I still think it would have been wiser to bring him straight up here after the Preakness and let him work on this track."

"The track wasn't the problem," Ashleigh said.

"He was handling it. You saw how well he pulled away in the stretch. The problem is he's tired after a long campaign!"

"That's part of it," Mr. Townsend admitted. "But I intend to have him shipped up early for the Saratoga meet." He spoke with authority. "A month at pasture in the meantime—and some light training."

From behind the Townsends, the first contingent of press reporters was approaching. Samantha was surprised it had taken them so long to get there. But she'd heard enough to make her want to leave. She could see that Ashleigh was still furious with the Townsends, and that Pride was picking up on the friction between his owners. As tired as he was, he was fidgeting uneasily. Samantha quickly rubbed a towel over his coat, sheeted him up, and without a word to anyone, started leading him out for his walk.

"I don't care what anyone says," she said softly to Pride as soon as they were out of hearing distance, "you ran a great race. So what if you lost the Triple Crown by half a nose; you're wonderful, boy!"

Pride wearily gave a small bob of his elegant head, responding to the tone in Samantha's voice. Samantha tried to shrug off her own uneasiness, but she had a terrible feeling that there were going to be even worse arguments between the Townsends and Ashleigh.

Samantha and Ashleigh spread out the newspapers on their motel beds the next morning and read mixed reviews of Pride's performance. Some reporters had given Pride his due for having run a great race; other reports, however, treated Pride's defeat as if it had been a huge one. Some writers didn't seem to care that only a fraction of a nose had separated the first- and second-place finishers and that Super Value had just come off a month's rest. All they cared about was that the horse on whom everyone had placed their hopes had disappointed them. Pride had lost the Triple Crown.

"It could be that Wonder's Pride has reached his peak," Samantha read aloud. "Like so many three-year-olds who show great promise early on, after the Triple Crown test, it's all downhill." Samantha slammed the paper down on the bed. "Who is this jerk of a reporter? How can he write garbage about Pride reaching his peak? How would *he* know?"

Ashleigh let out a sigh. "I hate to say it, Sammy, but that's the way racing is most of the time. When you're on top, you're on the very top. You lose, and suddenly your horse has all kinds of flaws—the trainer and the jockey, too. They start picking everything apart. I guess it's the same in any sport, and in this one, there's a lot of money involved. If your horse loses, it costs the bettors."

"But why don't they ever think of the horses? If it weren't for the horses, there wouldn't be any races to bet on! I mean, horses aren't machines. They're sensitive and intelligent . . . they can't always win!"

"I feel the same way you do," Ashleigh said. "Just ignore the stories. We know Pride hasn't peaked. All he needs is a good rest—and he's going to get it!"

Samantha crossed her legs on the bed. "I guess you're right, but part of what's bothering me is the Townsends—what Brad had to say. At least none of the papers said anything about him screaming at you. I'm just afraid it won't stop here."

Ashleigh frowned. "It probably won't, but like Charlie always tells me, don't start worrying about things before they happen. We'll have a whole month without either of the Townsends butting in."

"And we'll all be going home this afternoon," Samantha said with relief.

Pride seemed delighted to be back home again, even nickering for his pal, Sidney. The kitten jumped up onto Pride's back and started purring loudly as Samantha settled Pride in his stall. As tired as Pride was, the next morning he pranced with joy when Samantha released him into one of the paddocks now lush with fresh grass. He raised

135

his head to whinny to the horses pastured nearby, cantered across the paddock, then settled down to graze on the rich grass.

Tor called as soon as she got home. Samantha was so glad to hear his voice. He listened sympathetically as she described the horrible scene with Brad. "It's a shame you have to deal with him," Tor said, "but Pride ran a super race, Sammy. You shouldn't be disappointed in him."

"I'm not," she told him.

In school, everyone was wonderful. The kids and teachers who talked to Samantha about the race didn't have a single negative thing to say. They were all thrilled that Pride had done as well as he had. They were proud of the colt and Samantha's part in training him. Maureen, of course, wanted an article about the race for the graduation edition of the newspaper.

"It doesn't have to be long," she told Samantha. "I know you don't have much time, but everyone will want to read about it."

"I'll get an article to you before the end of the week," Samantha promised with a smile.

By Friday Samantha had noticed the great improvement in Pride. He hadn't eaten well immediately after the Belmont, but now he was putting on the weight he'd lost. He was even showing some of his old friskiness, cantering around his paddock and kicking up his heels.

136

Fortunately neither of the Townsends had been to Whitebrook since the race, though Samantha didn't think that would last. She cringed at the memory of Brad yelling at Ashleigh, but she quickly put it out of mind. She had the weekend to look forward to, when she would be going to the horse show with Tor. She was both excited and a little nervous.

Samantha was waiting eagerly when Tor picked her up early on Saturday morning for the drive to Louisville.

"This is going to be fun," she told him as she got into the car.

He smiled crookedly. "I hope so. It could be a disaster, too."

"Are you getting nervous?" Samantha asked.

"Do you have to ask?" Tor flashed another grin. "I'm already mentally calculating every fence in the course—and I don't even know what the course is going to be yet. My father's driven the horse van over," he explained. "I don't know if I told you, but he competes, too."

They talked horses all the way to Louisville. It was a beautiful mid-June day, sunny and not too hot, and Samantha felt so comfortable talking to him. Tor parked in the lot reserved for competitors behind the arena where the show would be held. It was a different scene in many ways from the backside of a race-track, but Samantha breathed in all the familiar smells of hay, leather, and horse, and felt the same kind of frenzied excitement in the air. Riders and grooms moved purposefully around the stabling area, readying horses and tack. Beautiful horses were everywhere. Some were Thorough-breds, some were European breeds or mixed breeds, and there was an Arab or two, but each was a splendidly fit athlete.

"Kind of crazy," Tor said.

"I'm used to that," Samantha told him as she gazed curiously around.

"We're at the end. I always try to get end-of-the-row stabling, where there's less confusion."

As they reached Tor's stalls, Samantha saw Top Hat's familiar white head over one of the doors. In the stall next to him an Appaloosa was gazing at the activity, its light coat marked by the distinctive spotting that distinguished the breed. Outside the stall, a man rose from one of the tack boxes and looked their way. He was an older version of Tor, and Samantha didn't have any trouble identifying him as Tor's father.

He smiled and shook Samantha's hand as Tor introduced them. "So you'll get a taste of a different side of competition today," he said. "Tor's told me all about that incredible colt you help train. And we've all read about him in the papers!"

"He's pretty special," Samantha admitted with a grin. "But so is Top Hat, from what I've heard and seen."

"Top Hat is quite a campaigner," Mr. Nelson agreed. "I think he and Tor will be bringing home a ribbon today."

Tor laughed. "At least my father's got a lot of confidence."

"I don't know if I'll be doing as well on Speckles here," Mr. Nelson added. "He's just coming into himself and needs more show experience."

"Tor said you compete in different classes."

"Right. Speckles and I are in a hunter division. Tor and Top compete in open jumping—much more difficult."

"Is he all set?" Tor asked, going to Top Hat's stall and scratching the big Thoroughbred's ears. Top Hat wasn't a terribly pretty horse, but his hindquarters were all muscle, and Tor was always saying he had a lot of heart.

"He should be fine," Mr. Nelson answered. "So, why don't you show Samantha around."

For the next hour they toured the stabling area and arena. Early divisions were already being jumped, and Samantha watched with interest.

"The fences are changed for the different classes," Tor explained. "Riders are allowed in the ring just before their class to walk the course. That's the only chance we have to judge the fences before competing."

Samantha nodded with interest. "We'll obviously be trying to get a clean round," Tor went on. "But we're also riding against the clock. The best clean round wins. It helps to be one of the later competitors, so you can watch the earlier riders and find out where the trouble spots are."

Tor showed Samantha the section of seats reserved for competitors and guests. "We can watch my father's class, then he'll keep you company when I jump."

"Don't worry," Samantha told him, "I don't mind being left on my own for a while."

They checked Top Hat, walked him, then returned to the arena to watch Mr. Nelson. He and Speckles did better than he'd expected. They had a very good round, with only two faults. Speckles didn't lift quite high enough for the last combination jump and ticked two rails with his back feet, sending them tumbling, but that still left them in fifth overall.

"My father ought to be happy with that," Tor said. "They did better than some more experienced horses." Samantha could see the growing tension in Tor's face and knew from experience that he was getting the nervous jitters.

"If you want to go down and start getting ready," she told him, "I don't mind sitting here by myself—there's plenty to see."

"You're sure?" Tor said.

"Positive."

"Okay. I'm better off pacing the aisle down there."

Samantha was so engrossed in the competition that the time flew by. She tried to imagine herself clearing some of the higher and more difficult fences, but couldn't. She had a long way to go before she could jump like these riders, though Tor insisted that she was progressing fast.

Mr. Nelson joined her, and they watched as the riders in Tor's division came into the ring to walk the course. "Hmmm, some of those fences look nasty," Mr. Nelson mused. "Those turns between the wall and the raised gate are incredibly tight, and he's going to have to be on his toes coming up to the water."

"The fences are so high!" Samantha exclaimed, staring at obstacles that looked nearly six feet tall.

"This is the advanced division," Mr. Nelson said, "but there's nothing here that Tor and Top Hat can't handle if they're 'on' and working together."

Samantha saw the intense concentration on Tor's face as he walked from fence to fence. She knew from her few classes that he was counting strides between obstacles, looking for the fastest and cleanest approaches. After a few minutes, the riders left the ring, and the first competitor entered on a black Arabian. Tor would be riding ninth, which gave him an advantage.

Samantha watched spellbound as rider and horse started through the course. She was filled with admiration at the rider's coolness and her ability to guide her mount. The course was not jumped in a simple circle. There were twists and turns and jog backs. "How can she remember the order of the fences?" Samantha muttered to herself.

Then, coming through one of the tight turns Mr. Nelson had pointed out, the rider misjudged and came up to the fence awkwardly. Her mount took down the rail, and because he was unsettled going into the next fence, he took down that one, too. The rider managed to steady the horse over the next several fences, but they were short going over the water jump and landed inside the tape line, which meant another fault. The rider left the ring to applause, but Samantha could see the crushing disappointment on her face.

The next riders seemed to have learned from her mistakes, but the tight turns claimed other victims. And those who managed to negotiate the turns seemed to be relaxing too much at the end of the course, getting refusals or knocking rails down at the final fences. When Tor entered the ring on Top Hat, no one had yet gone clean.

Samantha crossed her fingers as Tor saluted the judges, then put the big white Thoroughbred into a canter. Top Hat moved with the grace and excitement of a horse who loved what he was doing, and they sailed effortlessly over the first several jumps. Then came the first of the tight turns.

"Keep him steady," Mr. Nelson muttered.

Samantha saw that Tor was choosing a slightly longer approach than other riders had, but the approach brought Top Hat straight on to the fence. They cleared it neatly, sailed over a double brush, through a triple combination, came up to the water with collected strides, and landed well clear of the water's edge. Samantha heard Mr. Nelson's relieved sigh. Then they were into the next difficult turn. Again Tor chose a slightly longer approach, but their time was good. He didn't need to save seconds yet. They went through cleanly. Samantha relaxed a little, but there were still three fences and a big combination to go.

Tor and Top Hat didn't lose their concentration for a second. Samantha marveled at Tor's skill and how horse and rider worked together like one—though she knew that was how she and Pride worked. Tor and Top Hat went over the double gate, the oxer, through the triple combination that had claimed other riders, and soared over the last fence to echoing applause.

"They went clean!" Samantha cried excitedly. "They're in the lead!"

Mr. Nelson was grinning from ear to ear. "Very good round! But there are still four more riders."

Samantha saw the wide smile on Tor's face, and as he directed Top Hat out of the ring, he looked up in their direction and gave her a thumbs-up, which she returned. His skill left her feeling awed. He was a much better rider than even she had expected.

Now Samantha was hoping that the remaining riders would make mistakes, which wasn't very fair, but she got her wish. One rider managed to go clean, but her time was well off Tor's. A few minutes later, Samantha and Mr. Nelson rose to applaud as Tor and Top Hat rode into the ring to collect their well-deserved honors.

Samantha couldn't believe how proud she felt watching Tor sitting tall on Top Hat's back. As she watched him collect his ribbon, the grin on Samantha's face was as wide and as happy as Tor's.

11

"I CAN'T GET HIM TO CONCENTRATE," SAMANTHA SAID to Mike two weeks later as she rode Sierra off the training track at Whitebrook. "He just won't put his mind to it. I know he's got the ability . . . if only he'd stop fooling around."

Mike heaved a sigh. "It's so frustrating. He's definitely got the ability, but he's not making any progress. I don't know what to do. Maybe he just needs to mature a little more."

"That could be," Mr. McLean agreed. "His bloodlines certainly make it worthwhile for you to wait and see."

Mike nodded. "I've got Ms. Max and Well-spring coming along. Maybe we'll just put him out in the paddock for a few months and see what happens."

Samantha felt a stab of disappointment as she dismounted and patted the neck of the dark chestnut colt. She'd been hoping that she could find the trick to get through to the headstrong colt and get him to settle down, but at least Mike was willing to be patient and give Sierra another chance. She handed Sierra's reins to Len, who would untack and walk the colt. Samantha had already worked two other horses for Mike and her father that morning. Now it was time to take Pride out to the paddock and let him graze. Each day he seemed to get more of his old spark back.

Samantha couldn't believe how quickly time was passing. The last week of school had flown by. When she had said good-bye to classmates and friends on the last day, she had been relieved that summer vacation was finally starting. She'd been looking forward to the summer, when she could devote time to Pride, have Tor and Yvonne over for trail rides around the property, and work with her father and Mike training their horses.

But as Samantha walked into the barn, she caught the tail end of an argument between Ashleigh and the Townsends. Brad and Mr. Townsend hadn't been around much since they'd returned from the Belmont, and Samantha had hoped it would stay that way. But now, from the tone of the voices she heard, it seemed as if the peace and quiet around Whitebrook was already at an end.

"The Jim Dandy is the first weekend in August," Ashleigh argued. "That's too soon to race him. He hasn't even gone back into training yet."

"He looks pretty fit to me," Mr. Townsend said reasonably. "He's bounced right back, put on weight. I don't think it's too soon to put him back into a light training schedule, with the plan of shipping him up to Saratoga in mid-July."

Ashleigh continued to press her point. "But you want to run him in the Travers—that's the important race—and then aim toward the Breeder's Cup. The three weeks' rest he's had since the Belmont just isn't enough."

"He'll have another three weeks between the Jim Dandy and the Travers," Brad said shortly. "And we've already entered him in the Jim Dandy."

"Without asking me?" Ashleigh exclaimed.

"Frankly," Mr. Townsend said, "I didn't think you would have any objections. It's only July first. We have a month before the next race. I don't see the problem. We'll be leaving for our house in Saratoga next week, but I'll stop by here before then, and we can discuss the arrangements for shipping him up."

The conversation ended, and Samantha heard the Townsends walking down the aisle toward her. As they passed by, Brad ignored her, but Mr. Townsend gave her a nod and a smile.

Ashleigh was still standing outside Pride's stall as Samantha walked up. Her hands were balled in fists and she was staring blindly at the ground. "I don't believe them," she said under her breath.

"I heard," Samantha told her.

"I was afraid of this," Ashleigh said angrily. "I was afraid that they'd want to overrace him. I just can't believe Mr. Townsend would put money before the welfare of the horse—especially a horse like Pride. Brad's a different story. As long as I've known him, he's been impatient. He tried to force Mr. Maddock to put Townsend Prince back into training after an injury. The colt wasn't ready, and the Prince was Brad's horse—you'd think he'd care about his well-being."

"You don't think Pride will be ready for the Jim Dandy?" Samantha asked.

"Oh, I think we can get him ready," Ashleigh admitted. "But we also have to think about all the other races they want to run him in over the late summer and fall. It would be much better for him to skip the Dandy, get a few extra weeks' rest. Then he'd be in top shape for the Travers."

"I don't suppose you could change Mr. Townsend's mind," Samantha said, though she already knew the answer.

Ashleigh shook her head. "I may be half-owner, but I'm not even twenty-one yet. The Townsends have the weight on their side, and if I start too many arguments, I'm afraid Mr. Townsend will start pressing to have Pride stabled back at Townsend Acres. I guess all we can do, Sammy, is make sure this guy gets loads of TLC between now and the beginning of August." She reached up to pat Pride's head. "I'll go talk to Charlie about a training schedule—but darn if I'm going to start him this week like Townsend wants!"

As Ashleigh strode off, Samantha let herself into Pride's stall and clipped the lead shank to his halter. She could tell he was unsettled. The loud argument in front of his stall had to have upset him, and even the cats had deserted him for quieter parts of the barn.

"Come on, boy," she said soothingly to the colt. "We'll go out in the fresh air, and you can have a romp in the paddock and forget all this."

Pride nickered, but he was skitterish as Samantha led him out. Only after several minutes in the lush paddock did he seem to calm down. Samantha stayed at the paddock rail watching him until she was sure he was all right, then she turned and headed to the stableyard. She'd promised to meet Tor and Yvonne at the riding stable for a lesson, and her father was giving her a ride into town. She didn't know how she was going to concentrate on a lesson, though, with these new disagreements about Pride.

*   *   *

Samantha headed Cocoa toward the first of the four jumps Tor had set up around the ring. Tor had her jumping three-and-a-half-foot obstacles now, and she hadn't had any trouble so far. Tor and Yvonne were watching from the edge of the ring, as were half a dozen students waiting for the next class. Samantha tried to concentrate, her eyes focused on the jump ahead, but her thoughts kept going back to the argument between Ashleigh and the Townsends.

She and Cocoa cleared the first two fences, a gate and a brush, without a hitch. Then Samantha pointed Cocoa toward the next jump, a three-rail fence. The fence looked like a cinch.

That was her last thought before she suddenly found herself flying through the air over it, without a horse beneath her. Instinctively she pulled her arms in and knees up. She'd been thrown off enough racehorses to know how to fall. She landed on her side, her shoulder taking the brunt of the impact, and for a second she lay stunned, trying to digest what had happened. Then she quickly gathered her legs under her, stood, and brushed herself off.

Tor was hurrying toward her, and Yvonne was trying to catch Cocoa, who'd gone trotting off in the opposite direction. Samantha saw the wide eyes of the students who'd been watching and even heard a few sniggers.

She, who prided herself on her skill on horse-back, had just made an idiot out of herself—falling at an easy fence like the greenest beginner!

"You all right?" Tor asked with a touch of worry.

Samantha's cheeks were red with embarrassment, but she nodded. "I wasn't paying attention."

"I noticed," Tor said, giving her a crooked smile. "You'll just have to try again."

Samantha didn't want to try again. She felt like enough of a jerk, and she knew she still wasn't mentally focused. But she wouldn't have allowed a young Thoroughbred to throw her and get away with it, and she wasn't going to end her lesson with a fall. She nodded. "I'll try to concentrate this time."

"You didn't give Cocoa any leg before the jump, and he refused," Tor said as Yvonne approached with Cocoa.

Letting go of the reins was another mistake Samantha knew she had made, and she could have kicked herself. A loose horse in a riding ring or on the trail could be very dangerous. Samantha took the gelding's reins from Yvonne, threw them over his head, and remounted.

"Just the last two jumps," Tor told her. "Circle him around the top of the ring."

Samantha nodded. She knew what to do, and this time she'd do it right. She heeled Cocoa into a collected canter around the top of the ring, looked ahead to the jump, chin up, shoulders straight, in her jump seat. She concentrated on their approach . . . stride . . . stride . . . squeeze with her legs . . . give rein . . . and they were over! Samantha was already looking ahead to the next fence, a gate and brush. Stride, stride, stride, squeeze, release—and they were over that obstacle, too. Only as she circled Cocoa and brought him down from canter to trot did she let herself relax.

"Not my best lesson," she said unhappily to Tor as she led Cocoa from the ring to walk him.

"Everybody has a bad day—and you did great once you started concentrating," Tor said gently. "I can't talk now with my class waiting, but I'll give you a call tonight."

Samantha nodded. "Okay, thanks for the lesson. I'll talk to you later."

Pride went into training the next week. Charlie hadn't been any happier than Samantha or Ashleigh about racing him in the Jim Dandy, but he knew when they were up against a rock wall. "Better to go along with this than have the Townsends start making noises about moving him. We'll take it slow, and we'll manage."

Samantha started Pride back into training by riding him cross country over the lanes between the paddocks and down the trails surrounding Whitebrook. Usually, Ashleigh rode with her on one of the exercise horses so that she could watch Pride's movements, but one morning Tor and Yvonne came over to ride with her instead.

Samantha was in a cheerful mood as they set out in the cool morning air. With Tor and Yvonne keeping up a steady chatter beside her on their mounts, she could almost forget the Townsends even existed.

"Hey," Yvonne said, looking out into one of the paddocks, "isn't that the two-year-old you like so much. I can't remember his name, but I thought he was in training."

"Sierra," Samantha answered, "and he was in training. I was working him myself. I think he's got talent, but he won't concentrate, and he's incon-sistent and headstrong. Mike thought it would be better to put him out in the paddock and let him mature more before putting him back in training."

"He doesn't like running?" Tor asked.

"He likes running, but I have a feeling he gets bored," Samantha said. "He fights you every inch of the way until you give him his head, then he plays around."

"Well, he's not playing around now," Yvonne said.

Samantha and Tor looked over at the small paddock where Sierra had been put out by himself. The two-year-old had suddenly kicked up his heels and started galloping toward the white paddock fence.

Samantha smiled. "He's just showing off for us."

"I guess he is!" Yvonne said, lifting her dark brows.

As Samantha watched in amazement, Sierra galloped straight toward the fence and didn't swerve off at the last moment as she'd expected. Instead he gathered his muscles, and with a push from his powerful hindquarters, leaped over the fence, which was close to five feet tall! Sierra had flown over it like it was nothing.

"Wow!" Yvonne cried.

"Beautiful jump!" Tor said, staring after Sierra wide-eyed.

Samantha was thinking only one thing—they had a very valuable horse loose, and he was one of her favorites. Sierra had landed yards in front of them and was already galloping up the trail. Without thinking, she heeled Pride forward after the colt. Pride shot off in pursuit, and Samantha suddenly had horrible second thoughts about what she was doing. She couldn't gallop Pride madly along the trail. If anything happened to him, Ashleigh and Charlie would kill her!

But Sierra seemed to have more than a gallop in mind. He was out to play. He turned his head to look back at Samantha and Pride, slowing his pace and waiting until they'd nearly caught him. Then he dashed off again. They repeated the exercise twice, before Samantha realized what was going on. "He just wants company," she thought, trying to figure out how to out-trick him. When Sierra galloped off again, she held Pride back. "Let him go, Pride. Let's just keep to a nice, easy trot. I think he'll wait for us." Pride's ears flicked back, and he listened as he always did, but Samantha could feel his excitement. He seemed to like the game, too.

Tor rode up beside them. "I don't know what kind of speed this old exercise pony has, but there's a path through there. I might be able to come out ahead of that colt and cut him off."

Samantha nodded, and Tor heeled his mixed-breed mount up a narrower path that cut through the trees behind the paddocks. "What are you planning to do?" Yvonne asked, catching up to Samantha.

Samantha explained the game she thought Sierra was playing, and Yvonne laughed deep in her throat. "We'll get him."

Sure enough, as they came around the next bend in the trail, Sierra was looking back over his shoulder at them, ears pricked and ready to scamper off again.

"I think he's laughing at us," Yvonne said.

"He's probab—" Samantha cut her words short, because Pride was ready to go tearing off after the younger colt. "Easy, boy. I know you want to catch him, but I'm not taking the chance of hurting you. You're too valuable. Tor should be right around the next bend," she added to Yvonne. "He'll block the trail, so Sierra can't go any farther. Let's hope it works."

They rounded the bend in time to see Sierra skid to a halt as he saw Tor and his mount blocking the path. He spun on his heels to run the other way, and saw Samantha and Yvonne. For a second he rolled his eyes, and his nostrils flared.

"Shoots, he's going to run off into the woods," Samantha said under her breath. But suddenly Sierra's ears pricked. He tossed his head and danced on slender legs up to Samantha and Pride. The two horses touched noses. As Pride and Sierra sniffed, Tor rode up quickly and grabbed Sierra's halter.

Sierra immediately backed up, snorting and trying to rear, but Tor held firm and talked quietly to the colt. Soon Sierra settled down, although he couldn't resist trying to take a nip out of Tor's mount's neck.

Samantha let out a long sigh. "Got him. Do you think you can get him back?" she asked Tor.

"No prob," he said.

Len and Charlie were out in the stableyard when they returned. "What's he doing here?" Len asked, confused. "I just put him out in the paddock an hour ago."

"He jumped the fence," Samantha explained, giving both men all the details.

"Full of it, aren't you, you little bugger," Len said affectionately as he clipped a lead shank to Sierra's halter. The colt tossed his head. "Eh, don't you try biting me, or you'll get one back!" Len added sternly.

Tor was laughing. "Is that what you do to a biter? Bite him back?"

"I've been known to. Doesn't always work." Len grinned, then turned to the colt. "Guess I can't put you back in the paddock again right off. Too bad you don't show that kind of stuff on the track."

As Len led Sierra off, Tor turned to Samantha. "The way he went over that fence . . . maybe he's not meant to be a flat racer."

"What do you mean?" Samantha asked.

"I mean, maybe he should be trained to jump. Maybe that would hold his interest."

"Mike doesn't know anything about jumping, and I'm sure he doesn't want to sell Sierra."

"What about steeplechasing?" Yvonne asked. "Have you ever thought of that?"

"I haven't, no," Samantha answered thoughtfully. "I know there are quite a few steeplechase races at the tracks, but I don't know anyone who's trained horses for it."

"Maybe you should start thinking about it," Yvonne said. "Tor and I could help. Right, Tor?"

His blue eyes were looking very bright as he gazed at Samantha. "Right."

"I'll have to talk to Mike," Samantha said. "I mean, it's his colt. And Sierra might still come around as a flat racer."

"Well, it doesn't hurt to think about it," Yvonne said.

12

SAMANTHA GRADUALLY INTENSIFIED PRIDE'S TRAINING over the next two weeks, and by mid-July, when he was due to be shipped to Saratoga in New York, he was in the best shape possible. Samantha rode up to the track in the van with Pride, Ashleigh, and Charlie. She'd been to Saratoga before and loved the old track. People often had picnics on the tree-shaded grounds behind the grandstands, and there was always a special feeling in the air of friendliness combined with excitement. Saratoga was kind of like Keeneland, which was another down-home track where some incredible races were run.

Pride started his training in Saratoga very well, if not spectacularly. Samantha knew that he would

159

have benefited from a few more weeks of rest, but he was showing the heart and willingness that made him special.

Unfortunately, the Townsends and Lavinia were constantly around, since the Townsends had their summer home right in town. Barely anything could be done without them watching or interfering. Mr. Townsend wasn't as bad as Brad, but Samantha hated that someone was always watching her every move, and in general, the Townsends' presence created an atmosphere of uneasiness and tension.

The press people didn't leave them alone either. Like the Townsends, the sports reporters and track handicappers anticipated a big win from Pride in the Jim Dandy. And they expected that win would lead to a bigger win in the Travers three weeks later at the end of August. A week before the Jim Dandy, Samantha overheard two handicappers talking.

"Wonder's Pride is going to annihilate the field in the Jim Dandy," one said.

"You so sure about that?" The second man's voice was skeptical. "He was tired coming out of the Belmont."

"So he blew one race. He only lost it by half a nose. Look at the field he's running against in the Jim Dandy. None of them have been tested in the big races. He'll win it." The handicapper slapped a *Racing Form* against his leg. "No doubt about it."

But Samantha didn't feel as confident. She knew the horses in the Jim Dandy weren't necessarily plodders. They'd missed the Triple Crown for various reasons. Several had been recovering from minor injuries; others were only now showing the talent to run in the big races.

The constant tension between Ashleigh and Charlie on one side, and the Townsends on the other, was getting to everyone. Samantha could sense the battle of wills, and if she could feel the stress, she knew Pride could, too. He just wasn't himself, though no one else seemed to notice. Samantha wondered if she was imagining the change in Pride because she knew him so well. But even though he seemed to be in top form, Samantha just didn't feel good about the Jim Dandy.

She was proven right. Pride finished third. He looked good in the walking ring and post parade. He seemed fit, but when he got on the track, he never kicked in. Ashleigh told Samantha after the race that Pride never tried to grab the bit. When she held him off the pace, as she'd done in the Belmont, he didn't fight for more rein. And when Ashleigh asked him to run, he responded only halfheartedly.

When Pride came back from the race, he didn't seem tired, but Ashleigh was sure that was the answer for his poor performance. "I should have fought the Townsends," Ashleigh said angrily. "I should have flat-out refused to let him race! Now I don't know how we can get him on his toes for the Travers, and that's the *important* race."

Samantha nodded, but she thought there was more to it than that.

The Townsends showed up outside Pride's stall just after Samantha had finished walking and stabling him.

"What happened?" Mr. Townsend asked Charlie.

"I don't have any excuses for him," the old trainer said. "He came back in good shape. Can't find anything wrong with him. All I can figure is that he's still not fully back on his toes. I didn't want to run him in this race anyway."

"He didn't kick in," Ashleigh told Mr. Townsend. "His heart didn't seem to be in it today. I don't think we should have raced him either."

"That's crazy," Brad said. "If you ask me, it was the ride you gave him that was the problem. You're too soft on that colt. You could have gotten him going. I think it's time we had another jockey, who was out to win races, not to baby the colt!"

"What do you mean?" Ashleigh growled.

"I mean, you could have used the whip," Brad said angrily. "Wake him up!"

"Her riding's not the problem," Charlie told Brad. "He just wasn't on his game today."

"Then he probably needed this race to tune him

up," Mr. Townsend said, giving his son a warning look. "I just find it hard to accept a loss when he's won every race this year except the Belmont. I want him in top shape for the Travers, though. There should be absolutely no reason for him not to win that race."

The Townsends left a few minutes later, after both of them went into Pride's stall to look him over. Samantha's skin crawled at the sight of Brad standing in the same stall as her horse. Brad didn't care about Pride. All he was thinking about was money.

When they'd gone, Ashleigh turned to Samantha and Charlie, her face flushed with anger. "I can't believe what's happening! They want to get rid of me as jockey!"

"I didn't hear Townsend Sr. say that," Charlie told her.

"They've been talking about it—or Brad wouldn't have shot off his mouth like that. Mr. Townsend didn't defend me."

Charlie scowled, then said tightly, "I don't like what's going on any more than you do. Now that the colt's a star, they want to start calling the shots. Like we didn't know what we were doing getting six winning races out of him this year!"

"And all the fighting doesn't help Pride either," Samantha said, feeling angry and frustrated. "It upsets him. Can't you see that? He can *sense* things aren't right!"

"But I don't know what to do," Ashleigh said, close to tears. "It's me against them."

"I'm sorry, Ash. I'm not blaming you," Samantha said quickly.

Charlie sighed heavily, pushed back his hat, and scratched his head. "I can tell you one thing, we'd best get the colt on his toes during the next two weeks. If he doesn't win the Travers, we'll all be thrown to the wolves."

"And there's no way the Townsends will agree to taking him out of the Travers," Ashleigh said.

"Nope," Charlie agreed. "He'll run in it, whether he's ready or not."

The pressure on Pride and Ashleigh and Charlie was even greater now, and Samantha felt sick over it. This was no way to train a horse, she thought angrily. The racing headlines had pounded Pride. "Super Horse Doesn't Lift a Hoof." "Derby and Preakness Winner Puts In Lackluster Performance." "Wonder's Pride No Wonder Yesterday."

There were a few kinder comments, too, saying that the colt needed a race after his month's layoff. Others speculated that the colt had been raced too soon after the rigors of his spring and Triple Crown campaign. But those comments were in the minority. Samantha folded *The Daily Racing Form*, ready to heave it in the garbage, when one of the other grooms called to her.

"You've got a phone call waiting in the office."

Samantha got up and ran to the stable office, thinking that the phone call was probably from either Tor or Yvonne. She had given them the stable number, since she was so rarely at her motel room.

Tor's voice came over the wire. "Hi! I was afraid I wouldn't catch you. I'm sorry about the race."

Samantha was so glad to hear his voice. "Yeah, so am I. I would have called you guys last night, but I wasn't feeling very cheerful. The Townsends started in on Ashleigh after the race, and Brad told her maybe it was time to get another jockey."

"No! That's crazy."

"I know it's crazy. If anyone's at fault for Pride not doing well, it's them. They're the ones who wanted to race him so soon."

"Well, I've got some good news for you—at least I hope it's good news. I'm going to drive up to Saratoga next week with Yvonne. We want to be there for the Travers."

Samantha suddenly smiled. "You are? That's super. I'm so glad. It'll be so good to have my friends here—and there's so much we can do."

"I booked a room in your motel. Yvonne thought maybe she could stay with you and Ashleigh."

"Sure she could. There's an extra fold-up bed. Oh, wow! I'm so excited. When will you get here?"

"We're going to drive straight through and leave here real early next Thursday morning. Then we'll have the whole week up there before the Travers."

"I can't wait. Tell Yvonne I said 'Hi,' but I'll call her tonight."

"And don't let the Townsends get you too upset. Pride will show his stuff."

"I know."

Samantha felt much better as she hung up the phone and returned to Pride's stall. She'd missed her friends. Ashleigh and Mike were great to her, but sometimes she felt like a burden, always tagging along with them. It would be so good to have Tor and Yvonne in Saratoga.

Two mornings later, Brad Townsend showed up on the backside just as Samantha was about to take Pride out for a walk.

"Why aren't you working him on the track?" Brad demanded of Charlie.

"It's too soon," Charlie said gruffly. "He needs another day's rest."

"A jog on the track won't hurt him," Brad said curtly. "He needs to stay in shape."

"He'll get a jog tomorrow," Charlie told him with finality.

Brad didn't look happy, but he turned and strode off. His visit was a preview of how the next days were going to go. Every morning, the Townsends watched from the rail as Samantha took Pride out on the track. Having them there observing her and Pride so closely made Samantha nervous. She was conscious of her every movement, knowing that Brad, in particular, would pick on any mistake. He'd already threatened to replace Ashleigh as jockey, and Samantha knew she could be replaced as exercise rider even more easily. There were always eager young riders looking for a chance to show their skills. She just prayed Pride wasn't picking up on her own uneasiness, but he seemed to be going well enough for the time being.

On Friday, Mike and Samantha's father arrived with several Whitebrook horses. Samantha was relieved to have her father there. The last days had been awful for her, with accusations always flying, and the Townsends always trying to lay blame on anyone but themselves. His mouth tightened in anger when Samantha told him about the situation with the Townsends.

"I don't think I'm in a position to try to smooth things out," he said to Samantha.

"I know, Dad. I just feel so badly for Ashleigh. And I'm glad you're here."

"It's a shame that they're fighting," he said, shaking his head, "but that's what greed can do."

*   *   *

The next week Samantha started galloping Pride on the track. She worked him at easy gallops that would gradually build him up to the next race without stressing him. His strides were strong and sure, but his old spirit and vitality were missing. He wasn't running completely on the bit and he wasn't pressing her for a faster pace. He was doing what she asked of him, but no more.

"Maybe you just need a little more time," she said, patting the colt's neck as they rode off the track after the workout. Her voice was calm, but she was furious that Pride was being forced to run again so soon. He obviously wasn't ready. Samantha was more convinced than ever that the friction surrounding Pride was affecting his mental state. He wasn't acting like the horse she used to know.

Her frown deepened in an angry scowl as she rode toward Charlie, Ashleigh, and the Townsends.

"These slow gallops aren't doing him any good," Mr. Townsend was saying to Charlie. "He needs some fast works. We only have a week until the Travers!"

"This is the way Ashleigh and I have always brought him along." Charlie was scowling, and his voice was terse. "He's in condition. The object is to keep him there. We'll give him two short breezes next week. Too many fast works will take too much out of him."

Others who'd been watching the workouts turned at the sound of Mr. Townsend and Charlie's raised voices.

"He looked like he was asleep out there!" Mr. Townsend said. "I'd like to see him breezed tomorrow. And have Ashleigh work him from now on." Mr. Townsend suddenly became aware of the curious stares around him. "We'll talk about this later." He strode off to talk to Mr. Maddock, Townsend Acres' head trainer, who had several horses ready to go out.

Samantha was livid—not that she resented Ashleigh riding Pride. Ashleigh always rode him for his last workouts before a race. What infuriated her was the way Mr. Townsend had ordered them around. It wasn't like him. He had always been so reasonable and pleasant. What had happened to him?

She was so angry, she could barely talk when she dismounted.

"Are you going to do what he wants?" she asked Charlie through gritted teeth.

"Don't see what choice we have," Charlie said. "Townsend will be here. If we make a stink about breezing the colt, there could be worse fights in store. By the way, Missy, there wasn't anything wrong with your ride. I could see the colt didn't have any extra spark."

"I don't understand it," Ashleigh said. "Could

Pride still be tired? Or has he just lost interest in racing?"

"It's all the arguing and fighting that's bothering him," Samantha said, fighting back her anger. "I tried to tell you. Pride hears it. He's got to pick up on the tension."

"I think you may be right," Charlie said. "But I can guarantee the Townsends won't buy that."

That evening, as she waited for Tor and Yvonne to arrive, Samantha went to Pride's stall and talked quietly to him.

"I know it's hard, boy," she said, "but don't let it get to you. You've got so much to give, and you know we love you—Ashleigh and Charlie and me." She sighed. "Brad's always been a jerk, but I don't understand what's happened to Mr. Townsend. I wish I knew. I wish I could fix things. Now everyone's upset, and I'm afraid it's only going to get worse. I don't know what to do!"

She laid her forehead against Pride's neck. The colt nickered softly, and for a long moment she kept her head pressed against his warm body. "We'll work it out, boy," she said at last. Then she kissed him good night and left the stall.

13

SAMANTHA'S SPIRITS LIFTED WHEN TOR AND YVONNE arrived on Thursday night. It was too late to show them around the track, but they went in to see Pride before going to the motel.

"So did you have a good trip?" Samantha asked excitedly. "You didn't get lost or anything."

"We almost got lost because of my map reading," Yvonne said with a grin. "But Tor figured out pretty quickly that we were heading west instead of north."

They all laughed. Then Tor asked more seriously, "Have things gotten any better in the last couple of days?"

Samantha shook her head. "They've gotten worse." She explained what had happened the day before.

171

"But it's not fair to take you off as rider!" Yvonne exclaimed. "It's not your fault that Pride's tired."

"The Townsends are so desperate to win," Samantha said sadly, "that they'll try anything. And Ashleigh usually rides him for his last workouts before a race. I don't mind that. What I hate is the Townsends' attitude, and I don't think it's going to get any better." She shook her head, then added more cheerfully, "At least good things are happening for you, Tor. You must still be excited after getting a first in that big show last week!"

Tor flashed a wide smile. "Am I ever! Top Hat and I aren't done yet, though. We'll have plenty of work to do if we're going to compete in the National Horse Show in New York. I've decided to take the first semester off and start college in January. Even though I'm going to the University of Kentucky, I'll be traveling too much to keep up with classes."

"Your parents don't mind?" Samantha asked.

"They understand. Top Hat and I have put in a lot of work to get where we are, and competitive jumping is what I want to do for a living—both training and riding."

They talked for a while longer, but they were all tired and Samantha had to be up early, so Tor left for his room a few doors down the hall. Samantha and Yvonne were getting into bed when Ashleigh came home a few minutes later. She'd gone to the movies in town with Mike.

"It was good to get away from here for a while," she said sleepily. She slipped into the bathroom, and Samantha was asleep before she came out.

They were all at the track to watch the next morning's workouts. Charlie shook his head as Ashleigh breezed the colt through a half-mile. "Not the way I wanted to do things," he muttered to Samantha.

After Pride was settled, Samantha showed Tor and Yvonne around the track, then they went on a tour of the town before returning to the track for the afternoon races.

"I'll have to do some shopping," Yvonne said cheerfully when she saw the dozens of small stores lining the main street.

"I don't know if you'll find any deals," Samantha told her. "This place is a tourist town during the summers, and shopkeepers jack up the prices."

As Travers day approached, Samantha felt like a cloud was hanging over her head. Pride wasn't happy. Looking at him, no one would guess anything was wrong. He seemed fit and healthy, and his coat shined. Charlie had the vet give him a thorough checkup, and Pride received a clean bill of health. Yet Samantha knew Pride better than anyone, and she could see the change in him. He still lacked his special spark.

Brad had sharp criticism for Ashleigh as she rode off the track after Pride's final breeze. "You should have gotten after him more!" he shouted. "Woken him up!"

The day before the Travers, Samantha was still worried about Pride. "I almost wish Pride would come up lame so he wouldn't have to run," she said to Tor and Yvonne.

"The atmosphere *is* pretty intense," Yvonne agreed. "It wasn't like this in the spring."

"No, it wasn't like this in the spring," Samantha said sadly.

But as Samantha led Pride in the walking ring the next afternoon, she tried to think positively. Pride looked good, and the bettors, reluctant to give up on a hero, had made him the even-money favorite. Ashleigh looked grim as she got into the saddle. "Keep your fingers crossed, Sammy," she whispered. "I just got a huge lecture from the Townsends on how I should ride the race. They want me to put him right on the lead, and they made it pretty clear that they don't want me sparing the whip."

"You ride the way you see fit," Charlie barked. "Just remember *you* own half interest in this colt. Don't let them push you around."

"I'm just afraid of what they'll try to do if we don't win."

"Stop thinking about it. Just do your best."

As the field went out to the track, Samantha, Charlie, Tor, and Yvonne went up to the stands. Mike and Mr. McLean were readying a horse for the last race, though Samantha knew they'd both be watching the race on the television monitors.

Samantha had never felt the way she did before one of Pride's races. She'd been nervous before, yes, but now she felt sick with apprehension. Tor looked over and gave her a sympathetic glance. She tried to smile back, but didn't quite succeed.

A third of the way into the race, though, Samantha thought maybe Pride would break his losing streak. He was running on the lead, in perfect position for the stretch drive. But when the field moved out of the far turn, and it was time for him to change gears and really dig in, he did so only halfheartedly. He stayed with the leaders, but to Samantha it looked as if he'd lost all interest in winning.

'This isn't the Pride I know!' Samantha thought miserably.

Ashleigh did use her whip as they came down the stretch toward the finish. She used it sparingly, but Pride seemed to resent it more than anything, and he refused to pick up his pace. Others might have thought he was just tired, but Samantha knew better. His coat wasn't lathered; his strides weren't labored. He just didn't care if he got up to win, and when Ultrasound flashed by on his outside, he didn't fight back.

The four lead horses flashed under the wire, with Pride in fourth. Only a half-length separated them all, but it was a distance Pride could easily have made up—if he'd wanted to win.

Samantha closed her eyes, and her shoulders slumped. Pride had just put in the worst performance of his career, and no one could claim he had any excuses. Tor reached over and squeezed her hand. "Sorry, Sammy."

"What's happened to him?" Yvonne whispered hoarsely.

In the stands all around them Samantha heard the boos of justly disappointed fans. She just shook her head and sighed heavily, trying to blink back the hot sting of tears.

As Samantha had expected, the Townsends arrived at Pride's stall right after the race. Ashleigh had just returned from changing. Her hair was still wet, and her face was pale and sad. Charlie, too, looked miserable as he gave Pride a careful inspection.

Samantha saw from Mr. Townsend's expression that it wasn't going to be a pleasant scene. "A miserable performance," Mr. Townsend said sternly. "He had absolutely no excuses!"

"Nope, he didn't," Charlie agreed. "Nothing

that happened on the track, anyway."

"This can't go on. I've gone along with you and Ashleigh during this summer's training program, but obviously it's not working. I have too much of an investment at risk here. In his next race we're putting up another jockey, and we'll be taking him back to Townsend Acres to train under Ken Maddock."

Charlie didn't even flinch. He just gave Mr. Townsend a level stare. "Changing jockeys and trainers isn't the answer."

Mr. Townsend barely heard him out. "I've been letting you two run the show, occasionally against my better judgment. Now it's time—maybe past time—that I took back the reins. He'll be shipped to Belmont with the rest of our string."

Samantha felt like her legs were giving out under her. She couldn't breathe. They were taking back Pride? Ashleigh wouldn't be riding him?

"Mr. Townsend," Ashleigh cried, "he likes it at Whitebrook! Bringing him to Belmont isn't going to help. I have some say, too," she added defiantly.

"Ashleigh, I think I've been very fair in letting you have a say, but I'm not standing by while this colt's career goes down the tubes. He goes straight to Belmont to continue training, and Ken Maddock will be taking over." With that he strode off. Brad followed a second later. Surprisingly, Brad hadn't

177

said a word, but there was a smirk of victory on his face as he walked away.

Charlie swore angrily under his breath. Ashleigh looked devastated—as devastated as Samantha felt.

"This can't be happening," Samantha whispered. Tor walked over and put a comforting arm around her shoulders.

"I don't know what to do!" Ashleigh cried. She sat down on Charlie's deck chair and buried her head in her hands. "How can I fight them? I don't even care anymore if they change jockeys, but I don't want him back in their hands! I know Brad won't stay out of it. I know he'll interfere in the training, and I know his idea of getting a horse to do what he wants is to muscle the horse around."

A second later, Ken Maddock walked up. He was obviously embarrassed. "I'm sorry about what happened," he told Ashleigh and Charlie. "I just want you to know I had no part in it. Townsend just came and told me about the change in plans. I tried to talk him out of it. I tend to agree that the colt's been under too much pressure, but the Townsends are determined to head him to the Breeder's Cup."

"And they'll probably want to push him through two more races before then," Charlie said sourly.

"That's the impression I get."

"Darn them! It's all their fault," Samantha cried. "If they hadn't spent so much time arguing and fighting over his training, he might have wanted to run!"

Ken Maddock looked over to her. "You don't think he's just run out of steam, then?"

"No!" Samantha answered. "He's just upset by it all. He's not happy."

"I don't know," Maddock said. "All I can say is that I'll see the colt gets the best care and I'll keep the Townsend kid out of it when I can. I'm not so sure I'll do any better than you people, though. I think the colt's just burned out."

It was a somber group that went into town to eat that night. Mike and Samantha's father were furious at the Townsends' actions, but there was nothing either of them could do.

As they sat around a table at a small Italian restaurant waiting for their dinners to arrive, Tor turned to Ashleigh. "If I were you, I'd hire a lawyer. You need someone to represent your interests. I know you're not twenty-one yet, but can you get some help from your parents?"

"I hate to ask my parents," Ashleigh said miserably. "Pride has always been my responsibility."

"Tor might be right," Mike said, laying his hand on Ashleigh's. "There's a time when everyone needs help, and the way the Townsends are behaving, you do need a lawyer to protect yourself."

Ashleigh was silent for a moment, then suddenly she straightened her shoulders. "I'm not going to let the Townsends walk all over me. I'm taking Pride home."

"What?" everyone at the table chorused.

"Mike's leaving in the morning," Ashleigh said. "We'll put Pride on Mike's van and be out of here before the Townsends come to collect him."

"Look, Missy," Charlie said, leaning forward, "I know what you're feeling, but I don't think that's going to help matters, and you don't want to get Mike involved."

"I think it's a good idea!" Samantha said, then saw her father give her a warning look.

"Before you do anything rash," Charlie continued, "you go out and find yourself a lawyer. It won't be easy seeing them take the colt off to Belmont, but you can trust Ken Maddock, and Hank will be there. You can be darn sure he'll keep a hawk's eye on that colt, and he'll tell me everything that's going on."

Ashleigh shook her head stubbornly. Mike laid a hand on her shoulder. "I'm with you, Ash, if this is what you really want to do, but I think Charlie's right. It's better to do it through legal channels."

Samantha could see that Ashleigh was emotionally spent and close to helpless tears. She felt a cold fury at what was happening.

"All right," Ashleigh said, wearily giving in. "We'll do it your way."

By the end of the next week, no one had come up with any real solutions. Summer was nearly over. School would start in another week. Samantha was looking forward to it. She felt angry every time she walked by Pride's empty stall at Whitebrook. Sidney seemed confused, too. The nearly grown kitten sat in the aisle outside the stall, as if he were waiting, then looked up to Samantha for reassurance. "We'll get him back," she whispered to the kitten, picking him up and cuddling him in her arms. "I promise." If only she could feel so sure they would.

Tor came over one morning and drove Samantha to the Griffen Farm. Seeing Wonder and Townsend Princess, who was growing by leaps and bounds and was every bit as beautiful as her mother and brother, helped take Samantha's mind off things.

Charlie kept them up-to-date from his daily phone conversations with Hank, but what he told them didn't make Samantha feel any better. "Hank says the colt's really listless and going off his feed. Maddock is concerned, too, but the Townsends are determined to run him in a stakes race midmonth, and the Jockey Club Gold Cup in October. They've assigned another jockey, Chris Landry."

"At least they could have gotten a woman," Samantha cried.

"Landry's at the top of the national standings," Charlie said.

Samantha frowned. "I know, but it's not going to make any difference if Pride's miserable!"

"Well, Ashleigh and her parents have found a lawyer, I hear. Maybe that'll do some good."

At school, Samantha's friends rallied around her. None of them could believe the infighting surrounding Pride. "I thought adults had more sense," Maureen snipped. "At least that's what they keep telling us being an adult is all about. I think I'll write an editorial in the paper about greed."

They were starting their junior year, and Maureen had a lot more prominence on the school paper now. She'd been elected co-editor. Samantha had more say, too, and it was taken for granted that her articles on the horse industry would appear every month. She was too upset about Pride, though, to even think of writing a racing article. Instead, when Tor came over to Whitebrook one afternoon, she asked his permission to write about him and Top Hat and how well they'd done over the summer season.

He grinned with pleased modesty. "Sure, if you want. The sport could use the publicity. You're coming to the show at the stable this weekend?" he asked.

"Of course! Yvonne will kill me if I'm not there. But you're not jumping, are you?" she added with disappointment. How she loved to watch him and Top Hat perform.

"No, this is strictly a student show, but I think Yvonne's going to do real well. By the way, how's that colt who jumped the fence this summer? I haven't heard you talk about him."

"He's going back into training this month," Samantha said. "If he comes along better than he did in the spring, Mike's thinking of bringing him to the Florida races for the winter."

"I don't suppose you talked to Mike about training him as a steeplechaser."

Samantha shook her head. "No. With everything going on this summer, I didn't think of it, and Mike doesn't have the facilities. But I really think Sierra's going to come along. He's got something special, even if he can be a brat."

Samantha was in the crowded bleachers that Saturday to watch Yvonne take a blue ribbon in the Intermediate jump class with a flawless, faultless performance. Yvonne was glowing when Samantha met her outside the ring.

Samantha gave her friend a hug. "Great job! Perfect."

"I'm so excited!" Yvonne could barely stand still. "We really looked good?"

"You won the blue ribbon, didn't you? Yes, you

looked fantastic! I needed something good to cheer about."

Yvonne returned Samantha's hug. "Oh, Sammy, I know. But it'll work out with Pride."

Two days before Pride's next race, Ashleigh stopped by Whitebrook to tell Samantha that she was going to New York to be with the colt.

"I'm going to have to cut a day's classes to do it, but Sammy, one of us has to be with him," Ashleigh said. "I won't get a welcome from the Townsends, and I don't know if it will do any good, but I'm going!"

"Good! Wonderful!" Samantha cried. "Give him a kiss and hug for me. Tell him how much I miss him."

"I'll give him kisses and hugs from all of us. I hope seeing one of us will do him good. Hank says he looks like he's dropped another ten pounds."

Ten pounds wasn't much for a twelve-hundred-pound horse to lose, Samantha knew, but Pride had lost another ten pounds the week before.

On Saturday, both Yvonne and Tor came over to be with Samantha while she watched Pride's race on television. They both knew how anxious she was. As they sat around the TV in the McLeans' living room, Samantha scanned the screen for a sight of Pride as the race was previewed, but Pride wasn't getting the attention he'd received before his previous races. She caught a glimpse of him in the walking ring with Hank leading him, and Chris Landry in his saddle. Pride looked unsettled, and Samantha's heart went out to the colt. He was already nervously sweating, and his ears were flicking distractedly. *Oh, Pride, if only I could be with you*, Samantha thought in agony as she watched the unhappy and confused young horse. *I love you! I believe in you! I haven't deserted you!*

"He doesn't look good," Tor said quietly.

"No, he doesn't look good," Samantha agreed. "His mind isn't on it. I don't know how he could possibly win."

Pride ran worse than he had in the Travers. Samantha could see that he wasn't adjusting to his new rider, who handled the colt much more forcefully than either Samantha or Ashleigh ever had. Not that Chris Landry was mean. Samantha knew he was simply following instructions, and her guess was that Brad Townsend had given him the instructions. Landry urged Pride right up into an early lead, then slipped him in against the rail, saving ground just behind the pace setter. Pride actually started to pick up the pace on his own, but as they entered the stretch, Landry lifted his whip. Almost in midstride, as the leather flicked against Pride's copper coat, he slowed his momentum. Samantha thought of times past when Pride wouldn't have needed *any* encouragement to shoot to the lead. She or Ashleigh would only have had to release rein and use their voices. Now, Pride got the sting of the whip for encouragement. Samantha cringed as Landry used the whip again and again, stinging Pride's flank and shoulder.

"Stop it! Stop it!" she cried aloud. Her hands were balled in fists. "That won't work! Leave him alone!" Her last words came out in a sob.

But like a mouse, mesmerized by a poisonous snake, she couldn't take her eyes from the screen. Pride backed up further, letting two horses pass him. He finished a heaving, sweat-lathered sixth to horses he'd beaten easily before. The television announcer didn't let Pride's defeat go without a final, withering comment. "Three resounding losses for the Derby and Preakness winner. We thought he was tired; we thought he was raced too soon after the Belmont, but even the most faithful will now find it hard to make excuses." In the background, Samantha saw the fans jeering and booing her beloved horse off the track.

She burst into tears. She wasn't even aware of Yvonne and Tor putting comforting arms around her shoulders.

14

THE RINGING TELEPHONE ON HER NIGHT TABLE WOKE Samantha from a deep sleep filled with dreams of Pride losing and being jeered off the track. Groggily, she fumbled for the receiver. Lifting herself up on one elbow, she brought the receiver to her ear. " 'Lo."

"Sammy. It's Ashleigh. I'm sorry to call in the middle of the night—"

Samantha glanced at her alarm clock. The illuminated dial read three A.M.

"—but it's important," Ashleigh continued. "Pride and I are on our way home. I rented a van and took him out of his stable early last night. Hank did me a favor and promised not to say anything to the Townsends until morning. I'm about an hour outside Lexington."

"What?" Samantha said in confusion. "You have Pride? But I thought the Townsends—"

"After what happened in yesterday's race," Ashleigh said, "I wasn't going to leave him with the Townsends a second longer! Legally, I have just as much right to move him as they do."

"Are you alone?" Samantha asked. "How is he?"

"I'm alone. He'll be fine, though he came out of the race a basket case! I need your help, Sammy. Can you make sure his stall is ready? The others won't be up by the time we get there, and I'd rather not have too much confusion. He's already upset enough."

"I'll be so glad to see him!" Samantha cried. "I'll be waiting—and be careful, Ashleigh!"

"I will. See you in less than an hour."

The phone line went dead, and for a moment Samantha stared at the receiver, wondering if she'd been dreaming. Then she jumped out of bed. Pride was coming home!

Samantha dressed quietly so that she wouldn't wake up her father. She eased open her bedroom door and, carrying her boots in her hand, she slipped down the stairs. In the kitchen she turned on the small light over the sink and splashed cold water on her face. Then she sat on the kitchen chair and pulled on her boots. On tiptoes, she crossed the kitchen and let herself out the front door. The hinges squeaked, and she froze for an instant, but she heard no sounds from her father's room upstairs. She slipped out into the night and started down the path toward the drive. Night-lights were always left burning in the stable buildings, so she had no trouble seeing once she was inside.

I'll need bedding for the stall, she thought as she headed toward the storerooms in the back. *Hay and water.*

There were a few sleepy whickers from several of the horses, but they soon dozed off again. Samantha reached the immaculate storeroom, filled a wheelbarrow with bedding, and pushed it back up the aisle. Her activity had wakened the cats, though, and now they padded silently after her.

"It's okay, guys," she whispered. "Pride is coming home. You can curl up on his back again, Sid. I'm so happy!"

All three cats took up perches on the stall partition and started purring as Samantha forked the bedding onto the cleanly swept floor. She felt like singing as she worked. Pride was coming home! They'd been separated for a month, but in less than an hour she'd see him again! She could hardly believe it! But what would the Townsends do when they discovered Pride was gone? Hank would have to tell them that Ashleigh had taken the colt; otherwise they would think Pride had been stolen.

Samantha finished smoothing out the bedding, then pushed the wheelbarrow back to the storeroom. Going into the feed room next door, she cut the twine on a bale of hay, separated a sweet-smelling armful, and carried it back to Pride's stall. Sidney trotted along on her heels as she filled the hay net. Then she collected Pride's water bucket to fill it from the tap in the aisle. When the full bucket was in place, she put her hands on her hips and inspected her work. She smiled. Pride would have a perfect homecoming.

She checked her watch. The work had taken longer than she'd expected. Ashleigh and Pride would be arriving in about fifteen minutes. Samantha went back to the feed room and collected a couple of carrots from a storage bin. Pride had to have his treats when he arrived. Then she went outside to lean against the barn door and wait.

The eastern sky was turning pink with the promise of morning when Ashleigh drove into the yard. Samantha swallowed, trying to control her building excitement. As Ashleigh braked the van to a gentle stop, Samantha ran across to the driver's door.

"You made it okay!" she cried.

Ashleigh's face was pale from exhaustion, but she gave Samantha a smile. "We made it! I've never been so glad to see Whitebrook. Let's get him out!"

The two girls went around to the rear of the van. As Ashleigh released the latch and dropped the ramp, Samantha hurried inside. Pride was in crossties, facing forward, but he craned his head around as far as it would go and gave a nicker of pure delight.

Samantha threw her arms around his neck. "You're home, boy. You're home! I'm so glad to see you! I've missed you so much!" Pride nuzzled her cheek, and Samantha felt the sting of tears in her eyes. She unclipped the crossties and carefully backed Pride down the ramp and into the yard. Ashleigh was waiting with a lead shank. "Let's get you inside," Samantha said. "I've got your stall ready for you—and look who's coming to say hello." With tail high, Sidney trotted across to meet them. Pride immediately lowered his head and the two animals touched noses.

"What a good feeling it is to be here," Ashleigh said with a happy sigh.

They led Pride into the barn. "But what's Mr. Townsend going to do?" Samantha asked worriedly.

"I don't know and I don't care!" Ashleigh said. "On Pride's papers, I'm shown as half-owner. I called my lawyer before I left New York. He said the Townsends have no more right to make decisions than I do."

"All right!" Samantha cried. Then she added

191

more seriously, "I don't think the Townsends will let you keep him without a fight."

"No, I'm sure they won't," Ashleigh agreed. "I figure we'll see them over here sometime this afternoon."

Later that morning, after Pride was settled in, Samantha took a few minutes to call Tor and Yvonne with her good news.

"Oh, Sammy, that's great!" Tor said happily. "I'll keep my fingers crossed that you work it out with the Townsends. I'll be thinking of you. Let me know what happens."

"I will," Samantha assured him.

The Townsends arrived sooner than Ashleigh had expected. All day, Samantha had tried to think of arguments that would convince Mr. Townsend that Pride needed to stay at White-brook. She wouldn't be the only one defending Ashleigh's actions, of course. All the men on the farm were firmly behind Ashleigh. They'd all been amazed to find Pride back in his stall, but after the previous day's race, no one blamed Ashleigh for what she'd done.

Samantha was in the barn with Pride when she heard car tires crunching on the gravel. She ran to the door and looked out. Mr. Townsend and Brad were climbing out of Mr. Townsend's Jeep. Brad was scowling, and Mr. Townsend looked angry and exhausted. Ashleigh came out of Mike's house, with Mike and Mr. Reese walking behind her.

"I'd like to know what you think you're doing," Mr. Townsend demanded of Ashleigh. "Sneaking that colt off the track is theft."

"No, it's not theft, Mr. Townsend," Ashleigh answered firmly. "I'm Pride's legal half-owner. I've already spoken to lawyers. And I have every right to move him."

"Like heck you do!" Brad growled. "Not without our permission. That colt goes back to Townsend Acres. The van is on its way over."

"You're not taking him anywhere," Ashleigh said. "Especially after the way you had him handled in that race yesterday. And I know the jockey was following your instructions, Brad, because I heard you talking to him!"

"That race was a mistake," Mr. Townsend put in quickly. "It won't happen again."

"Where is he?" Brad demanded.

Samantha had listened long enough. She was sick to death of the arguments. Pride was not going to be put through any more misery—not if she could help it! She knew exactly what she was going to say as she strode purposefully across the drive to the Townsends. Ignoring Brad, she spoke directly to Mr. Townsend.

"Mr. Townsend, I've taken care of Pride since

he was a yearling. He's got talent and he's got heart. He's also smart and sensitive. I can tell you why he's not performing. It's because you're always arguing over him—fighting over when he should race, how he should train, where he should be stabled. He feels all that tension. He knows something isn't right. Of course he's not going to do his best when he's miserable. When people are miserable, they don't do their best either."

"I'd like to know what business this is of yours, Sammy," Brad snapped angrily. "Just stay out of it. Besides, we're not talking about a person here. We're talking about a horse."

Samantha ignored him and continued speaking to Mr. Townsend. "Look at what's happening to him, Mr. Townsend. His races get worse and worse. He's lost weight. And he's lost interest in winning."

"And what do you propose to do about it, Samantha?" Mr. Townsend's tone wasn't rude, but he sounded tired and unconvinced that Samantha could have a solution.

"Stop fighting over him," Samantha told him. "Stop putting so much pressure on him. Let him stay here and get a rest. You want to run him in the Jockey Club Gold Cup next month. Well, I think maybe he could win it. I think he could come back with all the fight he had before, if you'd just leave him alone."

194

"Why are you even listening to her!" Brad shouted. "She's a *kid*. What does she know?"

His father silenced him with a wave of his hand, then spoke thoughtfully. "I think Samantha may be right. After seeing the colt's race yesterday, I've been doing a lot of thinking, and I've come to pretty much the same conclusion. The colt must be feeling the pressure. We *have* been fighting over him endlessly. We've tried everything else—new jockey, new trainer. It hasn't worked. And Samantha knows Pride better than any of us."

"You can't be serious?" Brad cried in disbelief.

Mr. Townsend sighed. "Yes, I am serious. I'm tired of the bickering. I don't like what's been happening. We haven't been thinking of Pride's well-being. We've only been thinking of our own glory. Enough is enough. We'll leave him here. Ashleigh, Charlie, and Samantha can work with him. If he looks like he's coming around and is genuinely ready for the Jockey Club Gold Cup, we'll run him. But if he seems even slightly off, we'll skip the race."

"But he needs the prep for the Breeder's Cup!" Brad protested.

"If this colt doesn't come around," his father said wearily, "there won't be any reason to run him in the Breeder's Cup, whether he races in the Gold Cup or not." Mr. Townsend paused for a moment, then gave a brisk nod of his head. "No, I've made

195

up my mind. He stays here." He walked quickly over to Ashleigh and extended his hand. "Let's make peace."

Ashleigh looked stunned by Mr. Townsend's change of heart, but in the next instant, a smile lit up her face, and she took his extended hand and shook it firmly. "Peace," she said.

Samantha was beginning to tremble. She had just stood up to one of the most important people in the racing industry—and he'd listened! And because he had listened, Pride was going to have a second chance!

She glanced over and saw Brad glaring at her. Behind him, a Townsend Acres horse van was coming down the drive. Brad turned, then strode off angrily to meet it.

You won't need it now, Samantha thought and smiled.

Mr. Townsend came over to Samantha and shook her hand. "I think this is the right move, Sammy," he said. "Frankly, I've just about given up on him, but I don't suppose things could get any worse than they are. We'll see how it goes over the next few weeks."

When the Townsends and the van had departed, Ashleigh rushed over to Samantha and hugged her tightly. Both girls' eyes filled with tears. "The fighting's over," Ashleigh said. "I can't believe it! Thanks for speaking up, Sammy. Thanks so much."

*   *   *

Samantha couldn't believe how peaceful it was around the farm over the next weeks, but she *could* believe the change in Pride. When Tor came over to visit one afternoon, he noticed the change, too. He smiled as he watched Pride kick up his heels in the paddock, then he turned and gave Samantha a warm look. "You did it, Sammy. I get the feeling everything's going to be better now."

"I hope so," Samantha said softly, shifting her eyes away from Tor's to look out at Pride.

"So you think he might be ready for the Gold Cup after all?" Tor asked.

"Yes," Samantha said. "I believe in him, and if he keeps improving, I'm sure he'll do great!"

"Well, I believe in both of you." Tor laid his hand on hers for a instant, and Samantha felt a pleasant shiver go up her spine. She turned to Tor and smiled.

Over the next days, it was obvious that Pride was thriving. He was showing the spark that had made him a star, and the change in him was amazing. His heart was in it as he galloped during his workouts. He fought Samantha for rein, and when they finally breezed him, he burned up the track. He wanted to win. The old Pride was back!

Ashleigh's face was glowing as Samantha rode off the oval. "Let's go ahead and try the Gold Cup," she said. "He's ready. I think he can do it."

"So do I," Samantha answered, leaning forward to hug Pride's neck.

On October 10, Samantha watched Pride demolish the field in the Jockey Club Gold Cup at Belmont Park. The handicappers and even the most loyal fans had all written Pride off. No one believed he could come back. He went off at very long odds, but Samantha never doubted him, and Pride justified her faith.

Pride took the lead from the start and never let it go. Not once did Ashleigh have to urge him on. Pride had decided on his own that he was going to run his heart out and win!

The rest of the field, including Ultrasound and Super Value, never got within striking distance of him. He had roared around the track, firm on the lead, ticking off fractions that left Samantha gasping.

As Pride swept under the wire, seven lengths in front of the rest of the field, Samantha couldn't stop the tears of joy streaming down her cheeks. The crowd roared in delight. They were stunned, but thrilled by Pride's performance. Samantha and Charlie got rousing calls of congratulations as they went to the winner's circle to meet Pride and Ashleigh. Mr. Townsend came over to Samantha and took her hands. Even *his* eyes seemed a little misty.

"He did it, Sammy," he said. "I'm thrilled, and I want to thank you for all your help."

"I was only thinking of Pride, Mr. Townsend. I just wanted to see him happy again."

"Well, he obviously is," Mr. Townsend told her with a smile. "He ran an absolutely incredible race!"

Then Samantha hurried over to the horse she loved. Pride nickered a happy greeting as she approached. He lowered his elegant head, and Samantha took it in her hands and kissed his velvet nose.

"You showed them, boy," she whispered. "You're still a star. But I always knew you were."

In answer, Pride affectionately nuzzled her hair. The crowd loved it and gave them another rousing cheer.

▄ HarperPaperbacks *By Mail*

Read all the books in the
THOROUGHBRED series!

#1 A Horse Called Wonder—Is Ashleigh's love enough to save a sick foal?
#2 Wonder's Promise—Has bad training ruined Wonder forever?
#3 Wonder's First Race—Is Wonder's racing career over before it begins?
#4 Wonder's Victory—At last—all of Ashleigh's dreams have come true. But will she and Wonder be separated forever?

And don't miss these other great books by *Thoroughbred* author Joanna Campbell:

Battlecry Forever!
Everyone says that Battlecry is a loser who will never race again. Leslie is determined to prove them all wrong. But will Battlecry let *her* down, too?

Star of Shadowbrook Farm
After a bad fall, Susan has sworn never to ride again. Then Evening Star comes into her life. He needs her to help make him a winner, but can she overcome her fears?

- -

MAIL TO: Harper Collins Publishers
P.O.Box 588, Dunmore, PA 18512-0588

TELEPHONE: 1-800-331-3716 (Visa and Mastercard holders!)
YES, please send me the following titles:

    Thoroughbred
❏ #1 A Horse Called Wonder (0-06-106120-4) $3.50
❏ #2 Wonder's Promise (0-06-106085-2) $3.50
❏ #3 Wonder's First Race (0-06-106082-8) $3.50
❏ #4 Wonder's Victory (0-06-106083-6) $3.50

❏ Battlecry Forever! (0-06-106771-7) $3.50
❏ Star of Shadowbrook Farm (0-06-106783-0) $3.50

SUBTOTAL..$_____
POSTAGE AND HANDLING* ....$ _2.00__
SALES TAX (Add applicable state sales tax) ....$_____
               TOTAL: ....$_____
          (Remit in U.S. funds. Do not send cash.)

NAME_____
ADDRESS_____
CITY _____
STATE_____ ZIP _____

Allow up to six weeks for delivery. Prices subject to change. Valid only in U.S. and Canada.

*Free postage/handling if you buy four or more!   H0431